ZUKIE'S THIEF

CYNTHIA E. HURST

Zukie Merlino Mystery 10

© 2018 Cynthia E. Hurst
All Rights Reserved
Plane View Books

The characters and events in this book are wholly fictional and do not depict any actual persons, places or organizations.

Chapter 1

"If he doesn't get here soon, there's going to be trouble, mark my words."

Zukie Merlino slammed the lid down on the saucepan, something she only did under stressful circumstances. The contents were bubbling away nicely, but timing was crucial, and a few minutes more would turn them into an unpalatable mush. And since Zukie was rightly proud of her culinary skills, she did not intend to serve that up to anybody, least of all the person who should have already been in the kitchen waiting to be fed.

"I tell you, Joe, there's something going on and I'm going to find out what it is. Out for hours on end, coming home late, not saying where he's going, cell phone switched off – highly suspicious, don't you think?"

Her companion didn't respond verbally, not that she expected him to. At five months, Joseph Edward Lanigan's interests were pretty much limited to milk, naps, cuddles and a clean diaper. But he managed to look as though he was listening to his grandmother, which was all she needed.

"Aha, that sounds like him now. It's about time."

Zukie's sharp ears had caught the sound of a car turning into the driveway adjacent to her small wooden house. A car door shut, not a healthy slam but a discreet clunk, as if the person closing it didn't want to draw attention to himself.

As I'm sure he doesn't, Zukie thought. *As if I wasn't going to notice it's almost six and that he's barely on time for dinner.*

She was aware she was going to sound like a nagging wife if she said anything, and since she wasn't – a wife, anyway – she vowed to keep her comments to a minimum. The front door opened.

"Zukie?"

"In the kitchen." *Where I always am at about six o'clock,* calabrese, *cooking dinner.*

"Hey, that smells good."

As usual, Zukie's resolutions had a short shelf life, and she snapped back a reply.

"Don't try to butter me up, Lou. Another couple of minutes and you'd have been eating ravioli soup 'cause the pasta would have gone all flabby and the filling would have fallen out. And that's assuming I didn't throw your part of it in the garbage can."

"Well, I'm here now, so quit grousing. Hiya, Joe."

Lou leaned over the basket where Joe was lying, waving his chubby fists in greeting. He tickled the baby's stomach, making him giggle, and then opened the cupboard to take out two plates. Zukie watched him, glowering, as he put the plates on either side of the table and added silverware and napkins. In silence, she drained and dished out the spinach and ricotta ravioli, drizzled a bit of olive oil over it, sprinkled freshly grated parmesan cheese over the top and then set a bowl of green salad in the middle of the table. They both sat down, still without speaking, and began to eat.

As she dug into her dinner, Zukie asked herself for the hundredth time why she was so exasperated with Lou and whether it was justified. They were second cousins and had been sharing her house for more than two years since they had been widowed within a few weeks of each other. Spats between them were not unusual, but prolonged sulking was, since they both tended to follow the Italian custom of shouting and swearing for a few minutes, and then resuming relations as if nothing had happened.

But for the past two weeks or so, Lou's behavior had been what she could only describe as furtive. It was true that he was always up and ready for his breakfast at the normal hour, but then he tended to disappear for the better part of the day.

Discreet inquiries had revealed he wasn't at either of his daughters' houses, nor at Tino's Coffee Shop, his normal place for meeting friends. He had gone bowling as usual, but not to lunch afterward with his bowling buddies Dave and Neal. He had told Zukie he was off to play poker on a couple of evenings, but hadn't commented on his winning or losing the following day, which he usually did, so she wondered if he had been at the game at all.

He had even neglected one of his favorite hobbies of building model airplanes, the various parts of a small Lancaster bomber still laid out neatly on his desk where he had left them some weeks earlier. At least he hadn't left them on the kitchen table. If he had, Zukie's temper would have snapped long ago.

Of course, Lou was an adult and under no obligation to report his whereabouts to a nosy second cousin, but it still irritated Zukie that he was obviously up to something and she couldn't work out what it was. Short of trailing along behind him all day, she had no sure-fire way of finding out, even with her network of neighborhood spies. *I mean, observant friends*, she hastily corrected herself.

She was recalled to the present by a muted wail from Joe, who seemed to sense the tense atmosphere between the two bigger people in the room. Zukie scooped him up into her lap, balancing him upright in one arm while she ate with the other one. She finished her meal and waved the spoon in front of Joe, who watched raptly. He reached out and tried to grab it, making her chuckle.

"How's he been today?" Lou asked, obviously casting about for a safe topic of conversation.

"Good as gold for his grandma, weren't you, Joe?"

Joe gurgled in agreement.

"What time's Carol coming to get him?"

"She said about six-thirty, so any time now. Think you can hang around long enough to see her?"

Lou ignored the second half of the comment and cleared the

empty plates from the table, placing them in the sink. Washing the dishes was his normal contribution to the housework, so Zukie was pleased to see he was at least keeping to that.

She took Joe into her bedroom to change his diaper before his mother came to collect him, keeping one ear open for the sound of Lou splashing water in the kitchen, since she didn't trust him not to sneak out again. By the time she had put a fresh diaper on Joe, buttoned up his sleepsuit and carried him back into the living room, Lou had finished the dishes and was seated in front of the television, flicking through channels with the remote control.

Zukie stood and glared. She shifted Joe from one hip to the other and decided that as soon as he was on his way home she would tackle Lou. The knowledge that her cousin's activities outside the house were none of her business did not discourage her. That sort of thing never did.

When the doorbell rang, she was at the door before Lou could even look up from the television.

"Hi, Carol," she said, holding the door open for her daughter. Joe squealed happily at the sight of her.

"Hello, sweetheart," Carol said to Joe, as Zukie hid a grin. Carol had been complaining for at least twenty years about her mother calling her Sweetie, but she seemed to have changed her tune when it came to her own child. Of course, in a few years Joe might object the same as Carol had, but at the moment he seemed quite happy to be addressed that way. "Have you been a good boy?"

"He was absolutely perfect," Zukie said, handing him over. "We went to the supermarket and over to Colonna's this morning, and everyone said how cute he was. He takes after me, I reckon."

Lou snorted from the sofa.

"He had his lunchtime bottle and some baby cereal and yogurt, and then a nice long nap this afternoon," Zukie continued.

"So you think you can handle him every Thursday, assuming

you can take him around the neighborhood and brag?" Carol asked.

"Of course I can. He's a little angel, aren't you, sweetie?"

Joe gurgled his assent.

"Well, if you're sure, it would certainly be a big help to me. Then I can concentrate on my clients at least one day a week without worrying if it's time for him to be fed and without him crying in the background when I'm talking to someone."

"You make him sound like a nuisance. He's adorable."

"I know he is." Carol pressed her cheek against Joe's dark hair. "It's just that the way things are these days, it takes two incomes to make ends meet, especially when you have a child as well. Your generation had more flexibility."

"I suppose we did."

Zukie thought back, remembering how she and her late husband Eddie had had to pinch pennies in the early days of their marriage. She had gone back to her job as a waitress at the Plane View Restaurant once Carol was in junior high school, but that had been more a matter of choice than an economic necessity. Sitting around a house all day procrastinating about housework hadn't appealed to her any more then than it did now, one of the reasons she had invited Lou to move in.

"Anyway, thanks a million," Carol said. "I do appreciate you baby-sitting him, but I'll be off now, because Jim will be home soon. See you, Lou."

"Bye, Carol."

"Hang on, I'll give you a hand," Zukie said.

She picked up the bulky bag which held Joe's spare clothes, diapers, bottles and a few toys, slinging it over her shoulder. She followed Carol out to her car and waited until Joe was settled into his car seat.

"OK, what's up?" Carol asked her. "You're fretting. Is it Joe?"

Zukie was used to observing other people's behavior and drawing conclusions from it, and it was unsettling to realize this ability might be hereditary. But there was no point in denial.

"No, he's fine. Carol, I'm worried about Lou."

"What about him?"

"He's hiding something."

"What sort of something? A health problem?"

"No, I don't think so. It's just that he always lets me know where he is and when he's likely to be home and all of a sudden he isn't doing that. And he turns his cell phone off, too, so I can't call him."

"Maybe he's tired of you checking up on him."

"Oh, come on. Why would he suddenly be irked about that when he hasn't been for two years? He'd tell me if he was. And besides, I don't check up on him, as you put it. I always tell him where I'm going and he tells me. No big deal, except all of a sudden, it's like it's a big secret."

"No idea, Mom. My only guess would be that he's started to do something or go somewhere he doesn't think you need to know about."

Carol got behind the wheel and rolled the window down.

"And if you're smart, you won't make a fuss. You'll just let him go there."

Zukie watched the car pull away, debating whether her sensible, practical daughter was qualified to give advice on what could be a sensitive subject. She waved absent-mindedly, shivered in the evening chill and turned to go back into the house.

Lou hadn't moved from his viewing post, but he did look up as she came through the door.

"So you think this is going to work out, you baby-sitting Joe one day a week?"

"Probably."

"And you're the one who always said Angela was a mug for baby-sitting her grandchildren so often."

"That's because I didn't think I'd ever have any. Besides, Ange got married right after high school and didn't ever have an outside job, so I suppose baby-sitting is just kind of an extension of what she's always done."

Zukie always felt somewhat superior to her younger sister in that she'd had what she called a real job, the kind that produced an actual pay check, while Angela had thrown herself wholeheartedly into raising her four children and the grandchildren who had inevitably followed. Carol, on the other hand, had given her mother years of worry and frustration by waiting until she was in her thirties to marry and reproduce.

"Well, at least it'll keep you from worrying about me all the time," Lou said. "At least one day a week, anyway."

Zukie sat down abruptly and decided to ignore Carol's good advice.

"I don't worry about you. You can look after yourself. But since you've brought it up, I've got a bone to pick with you."

"Yeah, I thought you might. My first clue was when I found fifteen missed calls on my cell phone."

"So why are you turning it off?"

"Why are you calling me? You know where I am most of the time."

"I know where you *say* you're going to be. It wouldn't have come up except I went to call you from Colonna's yesterday morning to see if you wanted some more of that smoked ham. You said you were going to Vicki's house when you left here, so I called her, and she said you weren't there, hadn't been there and she wasn't expecting you."

"I got side-tracked."

"Sure you did."

"Why didn't you just call my cell rather than bother Vicki?"

"I did, Lou. Fifteen times. What if it had been an emergency?"

"You don't have emergencies, except when you're meddling in some police case you've been told to stay out of. If it was a real emergency, you'd call 911."

There wasn't too much Zukie could say to that, since it was true, so she decided to attack from another position.

"OK, you've made your point; it's none of my business. But if you're going to be so secretive, you can hardly blame me for thinking maybe you're going somewhere or doing something you shouldn't be. Otherwise you'd just tell me."

Lou ran a hand through his curly gray hair. "So you think I should just say, 'Hey, the mob wants me to stash a load of AK-47s in a vacant warehouse tonight, so I might be a little late for dinner'?"

"Don't be ridiculous."

"Or I'm planning to give up poker and bowling and become a priest, so I'm going over to St Augustine's to ask Father Martin for spiritual advice?"

"Even more ridiculous." She shot him a suspicious look. "You're not, are you?"

"No. And I'm not spending my time in opium dens, casinos or strip clubs, either. So just back off, Zukie."

Zukie looked at him, her bright brown eyes wide. The last time she'd heard him use that tone to her had been at least four decades earlier, when she had caught him and one of her brothers snickering over a pornographic magazine while smoking cigarettes they'd purloined from an older relation. She'd threatened to tell their respective fathers and been informed she'd regret it if she did. She had never quite known what punishment they had planned, but the tone of voice had been enough – for once – to make her button her lip.

But this was in her own house and he lived there by invitation, even if he did pay half the running costs.

"You threatening me, Lou?"

"I'm asking you politely."

Zukie thought it over. There were other ways of finding out what he was doing, so a graceful surrender might be the best policy in the short term.

"OK. You win. Don't tell me."

"Thank you. Do you want to watch one of your detective DVDs?"

Zukie recognized an olive branch being tossed in her direction. "Sure. How about one of those Poirot ones?"

"Suits me."

Neither of them mentioned the subject of the argument again and Zukie was just grateful that Lou had decided to stay in the house rather than leaving for the evening and telling her a lie about where he was going. She found herself wondering what Poirot or Sherlock Holmes would have done in similar circumstances and decided they probably would have deduced instantly what he was up to, where and with whom, based on psychology, clues or both.

I'll just have to work a little harder, she told herself. *But I'll crack it.*

WITHOUT Joe to occupy her the following morning, Zukie took longer to roll out of bed and head for the kitchen. She set the coffeemaker to bubbling and sat at the table with a piece of toast and a bowl of fresh fruit. By the time she heard Lou moving around in his bedroom and then the water running in the bathroom, she had formulated a plan.

She made scrambled eggs and fried bacon on automatic pilot, then dropped two slices of whole-wheat bread into the toaster. Lou's daughters were always complaining that Zukie fed him meals that were fattening or otherwise unhealthy, but Lou himself never said a word. She figured whole-wheat bread was at least a nod toward a healthy lifestyle, and after all, who wanted to live to a hundred if they had to eat rabbit food to get there?

Zukie poured two more cups of coffee, one for each of them, and sat down opposite her cousin.

"What you doing today, Lou? If you don't mind telling me, that is."

Lou ignored the dig. "I'm going to drop by Tino's and then I might go to the mall."

"The mall?"

"Yeah, you know, the place with all those stores."

"By yourself?"

"Yes."

Zukie waited for the invitation, but it didn't come. Normally they went shopping at the mall together, even if once there, they went their separate ways and only met up for a cup of coffee before driving home. It was clear, however, that Lou didn't want her to come with him this time. She did a rapid calculation. Christmas was over; her birthday wasn't until late summer and she was always roped in to offer advice on presents for his daughters and grandchildren.

Therefore, he was buying something he didn't want her to know about, or possibly, meeting someone he didn't want her to see. Or possibly not going to the mall at all. It was infuriating.

Still, there was little she could do about it, so she plastered something resembling a pleasant expression on her face and said, "Well, I hope you find whatever you're looking for. Or are you just browsing?"

"Just browsing, probably."

"Want any help?"

"No, I don't think so." Lou pushed his chair back and took his dishes to the sink. "Thanks for the breakfast. I'll see you later."

Zukie opened her mouth to point out he hadn't washed the dishes but closed it with a snap. She opened it long enough to say, "OK, see you later."

Lou took his jacket from the coat closet and headed out the front door, leaving Zukie alone and seething.

"That does it," she announced to the empty room. She picked up the phone and hit the first number on her speed dial list.

"Hi Ange, hey, listen," she said, when her sister answered.

"What?"

"I need some help."

"What kind of help?" Angela asked warily. "This isn't a police thing, is it?"

"No, I don't think so."

"So what is it?"

Zukie hesitated only a second before launching into her complaint about Lou's recent behavior. Angela listened without comment, which was unusual, but Zukie was too incensed to notice. She finished by saying, "It's probably nothing, but I don't see why he has to be so secretive about it."

"Don't you?"

"Huh?"

"Well, Zukie, he knows you're going to be upset."

"Upset about what? Ange, do you know what this is all about?"

The silence that followed answered her question. Angela might never have had an outside job, but any intelligence agency would have snapped her up for her ability to gather and disseminate information.

"I thought you knew," Angela said finally. "Everyone else does. Lou's got himself a girlfriend."

Chapter 2

Zukie didn't know whether to be shocked by the news or infuriated by the revelation that everyone but the person who shared a house with him knew about Lou's activities. It didn't say much for her detective abilities, either, which added humiliation to the mix.

"Who is she?" she managed to say.

"Her name's Shirley. Don't know her last name." Angela sounded apologetic.

"How old is she?" Zukie couldn't envision Lou being dumb enough to fall for some young bimbo, but men were unpredictable that way, so it was always possible.

"Fifties, I'd say."

That was a relief. "You've seen her?"

"No, but Karen has."

Karen was one of Angela's daughters and had inherited her information-collecting skills.

"And a couple of other people said they saw them together, too. They were at the supermarket."

That sounded serious and Zukie cringed. She went on to the next item of importance.

"Is she Italian?"

"How would I know?"

"You usually know things, Ange, even if you don't bother to tell the people it matters to the most. This Shirley doesn't go to

St Augustine's, does she?"

"No, I don't think so. She could still be Catholic."

That point wasn't too crucial to Zukie, whose church attendance could best be described as sporadic, but Lou was a regular at St Augustine's, and Zukie couldn't see him becoming involved with a non-Catholic. It was bad enough that his late wife hadn't been Italian, a fact that his immediate family had never let him forget, but at least she'd belonged to the correct church.

"And how long has this been going on?"

"I don't know. Karen saw them about a week ago."

"And you didn't bother to mention it. Thanks."

Zukie knew there was no point in asking for a physical description. Angela would either try to make Shirley sound unattractive so Zukie wouldn't be so worried, or conversely, try to make her sound like someone deserving of Lou's attention.

"Hey, how did you get on baby-sitting Joe yesterday?" Angela asked.

"Fine. Don't change the subject."

"Sorry."

"Ange, what am I going to do if he's serious about her?"

It was almost unprecedented for Zukie to ask her sister for anything but information, and Angela was duly flattered.

"Zuke, I don't think you should panic just yet. I mean, this hasn't been going on very long and even if he decided to re-marry somewhere along the line, it's not the end of the world."

"But I ..." Zukie stopped. She had been about to confess a weakness, which was that she hated to be alone, and in spite of a few annoying habits, Lou was a satisfactory housemate. It had taken a while to whip him into shape, but most of the time, he met her requirements. As for the more intimate side of life, she felt she could live without that as long as she had someone to talk to, help with household chores and accompany her when necessary.

"He didn't make a fuss when you were dating Bruce, did he?" Angela asked.

Zukie felt that was a low blow, and unworthy of Angela. She had gone on a few chaste dates with an old high school classmate before deciding that good looks and charm weren't everything. Bruce couldn't be relied on in a crisis, as she had suspected when they had been involved in the homicide investigation which had brought them together after a forty-year separation. And if nothing else, Zukie required reliability in her menfolk. So she had rather reluctantly told him that while it had been fun, she didn't think it should go any further, and it hadn't.

"No, he didn't, but that was nothing."

"What if it had been? It's your house, and I don't think you would have wanted Lou there if Bruce had moved in."

Zukie hadn't even considered that possibility, but now she turned her mind to various scenarios. Lou had sold his house to move in with her, so if he should decide to cohabit or re-marry, he'd have to find somewhere else to live. There was no way Zukie was going to share her kitchen with another woman, let alone occupy a bedroom next to an amorous couple.

And given Seattle's sky-rocketing house prices, he'd be hard-pressed to find somewhere affordable. She felt a little more cheerful at the prospect, until she remembered that Shirley might also own a house.

"Well, hopefully it will fizzle out before it goes too far. It's not that I mind him going out with someone; he's a grown-up and if he wants a girlfriend, it's up to him. It's him being so secretive that irks me."

"Yeah, I can see how calmly you're taking it."

"Shut up, Ange. Hey, do Vicki and Lynn know that their dad's back in circulation?"

"I'm not sure," Angela said, sounding regretful. "You'd think he would tell them, but then, you'd think he would have told you, too. I don't think you should ask them, though."

"Just in case they don't know?"

"Yes, because like you say, it could just fizzle out. Or someone else will tell them. They won't want to hear it from you, because you always say they don't trust you."

This was true enough, and not just because Zukie fed Lou the food he liked rather than what was necessarily good for him. Her theory was that keeping a man happy was better for him than nagging all the time about his health, a theory Lou heartily endorsed. There was also the small matter of the homicide investigations she had dragged him into, although Zukie felt those were not really her fault.

"I know they don't like me, but they're happy enough not to have him underfoot all the time. And let's face it, he wanted company after Bev died as much as I did when Eddie died. So it all worked out."

"Yes, it did." Angela was trying to be positive, which Zukie appreciated, given the many dire predictions she had received at the time Lou had moved in. "It may not come to anything, you know."

"Yeah, I know. Thanks, Ange. And if you find out anything more about this Shirley, let me know, OK?"

"Of course I will."

Zukie put the phone down with mixed feelings. At least she now had a handle on what Lou was up to, although she somehow felt his suggestions of mob involvement or becoming a priest would have been easier to deal with. And since he obviously thought she was unaware of his new interest, she had the upper hand, which made her feel a little more confident.

Her first impulse was to drive out to the mall and wait until she spotted Lou, since she knew his favorite places to shop and eat. She slapped that idea down as making her look both possessive and desperate.

Or she could search Lou's bedroom while he was out, looking for some indication of how serious the relationship was. She rejected that idea as well. It had been agreed when Lou moved in that their respective bedrooms were off limits, and the only time Zukie was allowed into his was to use his laptop.

That gave her pause for thought, wondering if he had e-mailed Shirley. Normally Lou used his e-mail account only for bills and ordering items, and even so, she didn't know the password to access it. So that was another dead end.

She began to pace the living room, which wasn't very satisfactory since she had to detour around the coffee table on every lap. Finally she gave the offending table a kick and collapsed onto the sofa, rubbing her foot and feeling thoroughly irritated with both Lou and herself.

"OK," she said out loud. "What's the worst that can happen? He decides to marry this broad and moves out. It could happen and you can't do a thing about it. So deal with it, Susanna."

She reflected that the situation must be serious if she was addressing herself by her given name rather than the nickname she'd been known by for most of her life. It was bad enough when other people called her by it, reminding her of childhood taunts of classmates singing 'Oh, Susannah'."

Voicing her concerns seemed to help, so rather than sit around feeling sorry for herself, she took her jacket and purse from the closet and went out the front door to her car. A minute later she was driving toward Colonna's Italian Deli and Bakery, a repository of good food and neighborhood gossip.

Zukie had been to Colonna's only the day before, but that had been more to show off Joe than to purchase anything. So she took a wicker basket from the stack and began browsing the aisles, inhaling the scents of bread, spices, salami and cheese, and keeping her eyes open for anyone who might have more information than Angela had been able to provide.

She tossed greetings to various people she knew from a lifetime of shopping at the deli, and collected cartons of sun-dried tomatoes, olives and artichokes, a loaf of ciabatta, sliced smoked ham and a chunk of buffalo mozzarella. Consulting her mental shopping list, she decided to pick up another bottle of olive oil, one item she always seemed to need, and then pay for her purchases.

Zukie expected to have a leisurely chat with one of the cashiers, and maybe learn a little more about Shirley, assuming the woman had ever shopped at Colonna's or had made an appearance in the neighborhood.

The last thing she expected as she rounded the corner of the olive oil and marinade aisle and approached the check-out was to come face to face with Lou, accompanied by someone who had to be the mysterious Shirley.

THERE weren't many moments in her life when Zukie had been rendered speechless, but this was one of them. She gulped, shifted her basket from one hand to the other, and then took a deep breath, as much to calm herself as anything.

"Didn't expect to see you here, Lou," she said, truthfully enough. "I thought you said you were going to Tino's and the mall."

Lou looked almost as pole-axed as Zukie felt, but he recovered quickly.

"I did," he said. "I mean, I went to Tino's and I'm headed off to the mall now."

Zukie smiled sweetly at his companion. "Hi, there," she said. "I guess Lou isn't going to introduce us. I'm Zukie Merlino, his cousin."

She had almost added, "And he lives in my house," but stopped herself in time.

"Oh, this is Shirley Minghella," Lou said. "She's an old friend."

Zukie felt like she'd been punched in the stomach. Not only was Shirley an Italian, or at least had been married to one, but she was sure Lou was lying about the length of the relationship, which angered her even more. The two of them had clashed on numerous occasions, but she could say honestly that she didn't lie to him. Misled him slightly, if necessary, but not an outright lie.

"Really?" she said. "Where do you two know each other from?"

She was pleased to see Lou's bushy gray eyebrows draw together as he fished for an answer.

"Not that old a friend," Shirley said, with a friendly smile.

"We met a few months ago."

Zukie was sure that wasn't true, either, but it was a little more believable than Lou's claim. She studied Shirley openly as Lou scowled.

Angela had been right about her age, which was probably not far from Zukie's. Mid-fifties, she judged, but well-preserved, with a trim figure that suggested frequent visits to the gym, and tastefully highlighted short blonde hair. She was wearing jeans and a black turtleneck sweater, covered by a smart leather jacket. Black boots completed the coordinated look.

Zukie knew without checking in a mirror that her own hair was a wild salt-and-pepper bird's nest, and her figure suggested frequent visits to the bakery. She was also wearing jeans, but they were topped by an old Seahawks sweatshirt and an even older parka, along with well-worn track shoes. She noticed Shirley's manicured fingernails and shoved her free hand into her pocket.

But this isn't a competition to snag a boyfriend, she told herself sternly. *You're only thinking of Lou's well-being, to keep him from being seduced by someone more interested in his bank account than him as a person.*

"That's nice," she said. "He didn't mention it. Minghella, eh? You must be Italian."

"I'm afraid not, Zukie. My ex was."

"Your ex? So I guess you're not Catholic, either."

"Zukie, that's enough," Lou said sharply. "Come on, Shirley, let's get going."

"Hey, don't let me hold you up," Zukie said. "Nice meeting you, Shirley. Will you be home for dinner, Lou?"

"Yes." Lou's glare could have stripped paint. Zukie ignored it.

"OK, see you later." She sidestepped around Lou and took her basket to the cash register, aware that several people were watching her with barely concealed curiosity. She smiled graciously as the cashier bagged the items for her and handed over her credit card. By the time she had finished the transaction, Lou and Shirley had left the deli, and Zukie let out the breath she had been more or less holding since the confrontation.

"Hey, Zukie." It was Nico Colonna, the older of the two brothers who ran the deli. She wondered where he had been lurking while she was talking to Shirley.

"Hi, Nico."

"Thanks for not making a scene."

"As if I would."

"With you, I never know. I heard people saying you didn't know Lou was seeing anybody and they were taking bets on whether you'd punch her lights out if you met."

"Oh, for Pete's sake, Nico. That's just what I needed to hear. So most everyone around here knew about it and didn't bother to tell me?"

"We thought Lou would tell you himself sooner or later. But I guess he didn't."

"No, Angela told me. I didn't expect to see them here, though."

"I gathered that." Nico grinned. "I thought you handled it pretty well, under the circs."

Zukie paused, then picked up her bag of food and with her free hand steered Nico to a quieter corner, pinning him to the wall under a framed poster of the Bay of Naples.

"What circs? Please don't tell me there's something else I don't know, some deep, dark secret about her."

"If it was a deep, dark secret I wouldn't know about it, would I?" Nico asked reasonably. "No, it's just that she kind of appeared out of nowhere and nobody knows much about her. And you know what people are like around here. You can't keep secrets, not for long anyway."

"So do you know where Lou met her?"

"No."

"You're no help, Nico."

"I only know she's been in here a couple of times on her own, and I think she and Lou have been into Tino's together. So I guess she might live around here. Or maybe not; we get a lot of people from other parts of Seattle who've read about us."

"And what about her ex-husband?"

"Not a clue. I didn't even know she had one."

Zukie sighed in frustration.

"OK, Nico, you can't tell me what you don't know. But the whole thing seems kind of fishy to me. I mean, Lou's a widower; he can date someone if he wants to. It's the secrecy thing that irks me."

She expected an argument, but to her surprise Nico said seriously, "Yeah, I see what you mean. If I hear anything else, I'll tell you. I like Lou and I don't want him suckered into something that's not kosher."

"Wrong religion, but I know what you mean. Thanks."

Nico escaped with an almost audible sigh of relief, and Zukie went out to her car. She sat behind the wheel for a moment, thinking. At least she had now seen Shirley and knew what she was dealing with. It was also clear why Lou had been attracted – the woman was good-looking and he was probably flattered to be seen with her. Why she was attracted to Lou was less obvious, but Zukie had her suspicions.

Lou had sold a thriving plumbing business when he retired, and then he had sold his house to move in with Zukie. She happened to know that most of the profits from both the business and house had been invested prudently, both to provide for his retirement and as a legacy for his daughters and his grandchildren.

It was the sort of financial security that a divorcee, even one who could afford leather jackets and blonde highlights, might well covet. And Zukie had to admit that although Lou was no movie star, he was quite presentable for his age. If he smartened himself up a little and shed a few pounds, he might even pass for handsome.

Since she had now determined what the attraction was on both parts, her only decision was what to do about it. Leave well enough alone and bite the bullet if he decided to re-marry? Or dig a little more and see if there was any good reason why Lou should back off before things got too intense?

Being a congenital snoop, she instantly went for the second option. If she was careful, she wouldn't ruffle any feathers, and since Lou was already mad at her, she had little to lose.

Having made her decision, she headed back home, put her purchases away and picked up the phone.

"Hey, Ange, guess what?"

"What?"

"I've met Shirley."

"Really? What's she like?"

"Fifties, blonde, good dresser. Says she's divorced. Her ex-husband was Italian, so I guess he's the one named Minghella."

"Minghella," Angela repeated. "I've heard that name, I'm sure."

Zukie's antenna quivered. "Think, Ange. Do you know anything about him? Or about her?"

"Not off the top of my head, but I'll do some research."

"Tactfully. I don't want people to know it's me asking."

"Who else would it be?"

Zukie had to admit that was a good question, but she rallied. "It could be his daughters. Or his brother."

"I suppose so. Well, I'll ask around."

"Thanks, Ange."

She put the phone down and thought for a minute. It was clear that Lou's daughters weren't clued in, or they would have said something. If they could object to her feeding their father white bread instead of whole wheat, they certainly would have expressed an opinion about his dating a divorced blonde with possible designs on his bank account.

So much as she hated to do it, she felt she owed it to Vicki and Lynn to keep them in the loop. She reached for her small phone book, where she kept numbers she might have to call in an emergency. This situation qualified as one, she was sure.

She had just located Vicki's number when the phone rang, making her jump. She reached for it cautiously.

"Hello?"

"Zuke? Thank God you're at home."

It was Lou, sounding thoroughly shaken.

"Course I'm at home. That's the number you called, remember?"

"Don't joke. Can you come pick me up?"

Zukie's eyebrows shot upward and her mouth opened and shut. She opened it again and said, "Pick you up? Where the heck are you?"

"At the mall. I'll be outside Nordstroms, the main door. Don't park, just stop long enough for me to get in the car."

Zukie couldn't believe her ears, but it seemed he was serious. She looked at her watch. "Give me about fifteen minutes, OK?"

"Right."

"You going to tell me what this is about?"

She thought Lou wasn't going to answer, but then he lowered his voice and said, "I could be wrong and I hope I am, but I think someone just tried to kill me."

Chapter 3

Under the circumstances, Zukie decided not to argue the point. Lou was probably wrong, but it was just possible he wasn't. However, at the moment it appeared more important to remove him from the scene, attempted murder or not.

So she said only, "Right, I'll be there as soon as I can."

"Thanks."

She hung up and reached for her jacket and purse again. As she went out to the driveway, she found a moment to wonder where Shirley had gone. They had set off from Colonna's together, although she hadn't seen whose car they were in. She had assumed it was Lou's Buick, but if so, why couldn't he drive it back from the mall?

Zukie started to back out of the driveway, glancing up and down the street in case the mysterious would-be assassin knew where Lou lived. But she saw only her next-door neighbor Shelly Ryder, shaking out a throw rug on the front porch.

Zukie braked and rolled down the window.

"Shelly! You got a minute?"

Shelly came over to the car. "What's up?"

"Can you spare a few minutes and come out to the mall with me? It's not to go shopping and we won't stay long, but it's important."

One of the things Zukie liked about Shelly was that she didn't waste time with silly questions. She took one look at Zukie's face and said, "Sure. I don't need to pick the kids up until three."

"Good. Get in."

"Give me a sec and I'll lock the front door," Shelly said, and hurried back to the porch. Two minutes later she was in the passenger seat beside Zukie, who shot off down the quiet street as if pursued by a squad of armed attackers.

It wasn't until they were on the freeway that Zukie said, "I suppose you're wondering what this is all about."

"That did cross my mind, yes."

Zukie took a deep breath and launched into a surprisingly coherent recital of the events of the past few days. Surprising, because her narratives usually tended to wander off onto numerous side paths before eventually circling around to rejoin the main story. She ended by saying, "So I don't know what happened, where Shirley is or where his car is."

"Bizarre," Shelly said.

"You're telling me. And when I saw you, it occurred to me it might be a good idea to have someone else along, in case he can't get to his car or something. You could drive mine back and I'd get his."

"All right."

"Or you might have to go find him, if he's not where he said he'd be." She chewed a fingernail nervously.

"Zukie, he'll be all right. He probably just imagined the part about someone trying to kill him."

"Don't think so, Shelly. He sounded really rattled and that's not like Lou. He's the one always telling me to calm down and stop exaggerating."

She took the exit to the mall and swore at the red light that held her up a few blocks away. When it changed to green, she floored the accelerator and Shelly said, "Take it easy. It won't help Lou if you have an accident before you get there."

Zukie ignored this good advice and swung around the corner into the mall parking lot. She slowed down then, cruising along as if looking for a parking place. As she approached the department store entrance where Lou had said he'd be waiting, she slowed even further, and Shelly peered out of the passenger side window.

"There he is," she said suddenly.

"Is he OK?"

"He's with somebody. Can't see who. Yes, I can. Looks like a paramedic-type person."

"Holy saints. Is Lou on his feet?"

"Yes. Stop here, and I'll go get him. You can loop round and come back to pick us up. If anyone asks, I'll say I'm his wife."

"His daughter, Shelly. You're thirty years younger than he is."

"Details, details. Let me get out."

Zukie stopped the car just long enough for Shelly to hop out, and then made another loop of the parking lot. She pulled up in front of the department store loading bay to see Shelly holding Lou's arm as an attentive, concerned daughter would, and guiding him toward the curb. They got in the car – Lou in the front and Shelly in the back seat – and Zukie accelerated away.

They had covered the length of the long parking lot before Zukie pulled into a space which didn't have cars on either side. She cut the engine and turned to look at her passenger.

"What the hell happened back there, Lou? Where's your car? Are you OK?"

Lou answered the questions in reverse order. "More or less, yeah. My car's in the parking garage. I still don't know exactly what happened."

"Why was there a paramedic with you?"

"Because I got slammed into the fender of a parked car in the garage by some idiot. If I'd fallen the other way, I'd have gone under his wheels. The paramedic was there because someone called 911, I guess."

Zukie took a closer look. The sleeve of Lou's jacket was ripped and his wrist and hand were bruised. One of his pants legs was filthy down the side, as if it had been dragged through grease or mud. She shifted her gaze upward, but his head and face seemed untouched.

"Where's Shirley?"

"Damned if I know."

That was the most encouraging thing Zukie had heard him say for days. She decided it was safe to probe a little further.

"Did you go to the mall together?"

"Yeah. We were going to just take a look around a couple stores and then go for lunch."

"So what ..."

"Shut up and I'll tell you. We got to the mall and looked around. Everything was fine. We decided where we were going to have lunch and went to the restaurant. Then Shirley said she'd left her reading glasses in my car and would I mind going to get them so she could read the menu."

"Had she left them there?"

"Good question. She does wear reading glasses, I know. Anyway, being a gentleman, I said, sure, and went back to the parking garage."

Zukie held up a cautioning hand.

"Lou, you never park in the garage. You don't like it. You always park out in the open lot."

"I know."

"So parking there was her idea?"

"Yeah, so we could walk across the bridge thing and not get wet."

"It wasn't raining."

"Will you stop interrupting me? So I parked in the garage like she suggested. No big deal. And I went back to the garage to look for her glasses."

He paused and glared, as if daring Zukie to raise an objection.

"I was almost back to my car when this car came speeding around the corner, aiming straight at me, or it seemed to be, anyway. The fender hit my leg and knocked me into a parked car. I landed on my butt and a couple of people came over to see if I was OK. I think one of them called either 911 or the mall security people. Anyway, a paramedic turned up a few minutes later to check me out."

"You're lucky you didn't break a leg," Zukie said.

"I'm lucky I was walking so close to the parked cars. If I'd been walking down the middle of the row they would have run over me instead of just winging me."

"Did you get any details of the car or the driver?" Shelly asked, and Zukie nodded in approval at the sensible question.

"Not much. A black Ford sedan. Washington plates, I'm pretty sure, but I didn't get the number at all. Nutcase driver, a guy."

Zukie asked the question she had been thinking about since Lou's initial phone call.

"Do you think it was deliberate?"

"I don't know what to think. It seemed like it was. But why me?"

"That's a dumb question," Zukie said. "Because you were with Shirley, obviously. She sent you back there so somebody could take a shot at you. Speaking of Shirley, where do you reckon she is? I don't think she's patiently waiting in the restaurant for you to come back with her glasses, not after half an hour or so."

"No, I don't think so, either."

"Unless she hopes you're dead and is sitting there listening for sirens."

"Aren't you the little ray of sunshine."

"I suppose we could go to the restaurant and check," Shelly said.

"Don't bother," Lou said. "OK, Zukie, go ahead and say it. I guess I've been a sucker who's been taken for a ride and now I've got some homicidal nut after me."

"Could be. The question is why."

"I don't know, honest to God."

"Right, we can discuss that later. You still got your car keys?"

Lou groped in his pocket. "Yeah."

"Good. We'll head back in the direction of the garage and I'll go get your car."

"No, I will," Shelly said. "Zukie, you told me you met Shirley this morning at Colonna's. So she knows what you look like and she'd guess Lou might have called you. She doesn't know me. Even if she or someone is watching Lou's car, which I doubt, they won't realize that's where I'm going until it's too late. Where are you parked, Lou?"

"Second level, not far from the bridge. First row."

Zukie had to admit this plan had its advantages.

"OK, Shelly, but be careful. I'll wait just outside the garage until you drive out and follow you home. If there's any problem at all, leave the car and call me."

"Right."

Lou handed the keys to Shelly and Zukie drove back, dropping her at the entrance to the parking garage and parking where she could watch it. She chewed her fingernails until she saw Lou's Buick, with Shelly at the wheel, coming toward them, and then started the engine.

"Stay behind her," Lou said. "Keep her in sight."

"I know what I'm doing, Lou. If a black Ford follows her, I'm on it."

"Saints preserve us. I'd have been better off getting run over."

But the possible car chase never materialized, much to Lou's obvious relief. Shelly drove steadily, at a speed calculated not to attract attention, and Zukie followed a discreet distance behind.

No black Ford appeared, but she didn't fully relax until they'd taken the exit up to Beacon Hill and approached their respective houses. Shelly drove into Zukie's driveway and parked the Buick, and Zukie pulled up behind her.

"Go change your clothes and clean yourself up," she ordered Lou. "Then we'll try and work out what the heck is going on here."

For once Lou didn't argue. He hobbled up to the front door and let himself in. Shelly came over and said, "What is this, Zukie? Do you think Lou was deliberately targeted?"

"Looks like it. Can't just be coincidence Shirley sent him back to the car, which was parked in a place he normally wouldn't park, and then someone tries to run over him."

"I agree. Do you want me to come over?"

"Not yet. Let me talk to him first."

"Right. I'm here if you need back-up."

"Thanks, Shelly. You're a star."

Zukie took the Buick's keys from Shelly and went back in the house, where the sound of running water told her Lou was following her instructions. She filled the coffeemaker, on the theory that he would need stimulation first, followed by the lunch he had been forced to skip.

By the time he appeared in the kitchen, washed and wearing clean clothes, she had made him a hearty ham and cheese sandwich and poured a large cup of strong Italian coffee. Lou gave her a grateful glance and sat down at the table.

Neither of them spoke until the sandwich and the first cup of coffee had disappeared. Then Lou said, "Thanks for not telling me what an idiot I've been."

Zukie had been about to say something of the sort, but now she looked at his unhappy expression and changed her tune.

"Heck, Lou, you were lonely and wanted company and something else, too. I mean, you've got me and your girls and your friends, but I'm not stupid. There's one thing none of us could give you and I'm guessing Shirley did. So that's why you didn't want to tell me or Lynn or Vicki that you were seeing her. You thought we'd give you some big morality lecture. We wouldn't have – or at least I wouldn't have – but you probably weren't thinking straight. Men don't in that situation. Am I right?"

Lou nodded silently.

"OK, now that's out in the open, we can move on. You can leave out the private bits, but tell me everything else you know about Shirley."

"Why?"

"Lou, the woman tried to kill you. Or have you killed. Don't you want to know why?"

"Not really. I won't be seeing her again, obviously."

"Don't count on it," Zukie said grimly. "Now start talking."

Lou drained his second cup of coffee and said, "Are you thinking of doing some kind of investigation, Zuke? Because I'm OK, so I think it would be better to drop it."

"From what you've said, it was attempted murder. If you won't help me, I'll go to Jim, and at least report it."

Lou looked across the table and realized his cousin meant what she said. She had been terminally inquisitive even before meeting homicide detective Jim Lanigan, but becoming involved in several investigations and then acquiring Lanigan as a son-in-law had brought out all her previously concealed talents. Lou knew Lanigan and his immediate superior regarded her technique as a combination of intelligence, luck, stubbornness and possibly witchcraft, but they couldn't deny she had been successful.

"OK, I'll tell you what I know, but don't make a big deal out of it. And if nothing else happens, you don't need to involve Jim."

"Let me be the judge of that," Zukie said sternly. "Right. Start at the beginning. When and where did you meet her?"

For a minute she thought Lou wasn't going to tell her, but then he said, "I met her about a month ago, maybe a little more, at the bowling alley."

"You're not telling me she bowls, are you? She'd wreck her manicure."

Lou glared. "I never said she bowled. She was in the parking lot and her car battery was dead. She'd been in that convenience store on the other side of the lot, next to the Plane View. I hooked up my jump leads so she could get it started."

"You fell for one of the oldest tricks in the book. Go on."

"So she offered to buy me a coffee at the Plane View by way of thanking me. What was the harm in that?"

Zukie refrained from comment, although she could have pointed out that if she'd still been working at the Plane View restaurant, none of this would have happened.

Lou continued, "She was good-looking and seemed pretty

nice, so we got to talking, and before I knew it, I'd asked her out for lunch. And, um, one thing kind of led to another."

"OK, I get the picture. What did she say about herself?"

"Not too much. She said she was divorced and lived in Georgetown. No kids. There wasn't any reason not to believe her."

"Did she say anything about her ex-husband?"

"No."

"Like what his name was?"

"Minghella, I guess, but I don't know his first name. No, wait. Mike. Mick. Something like that. What does it matter?"

"It matters if he's the guy who tried to run over you."

"Why would he? They were divorced."

"So she said. Maybe they were; maybe they weren't. Or maybe he didn't like the idea of her going out with someone else. But that doesn't make sense, either, since she's the one who set you up by sending you back to the car. And she targeted you in the first place at the bowling alley. So they're working together."

Zukie drummed the table with her fingers, trying to make sense of the known facts. It wasn't easy.

"Did she say anything about having a job? I wouldn't think she did, not if she could hang around bowling alleys and go to the mall for lunch."

"I think she said she'd quit working. I don't know why."

"Did you ever go to her house?"

"No."

"So where did you … "

"Ever hear of motels, Zuke?"

"Jeez, Lou, that's so sleazy. And kind of odd, now that I think of it. Why didn't you go to her house?"

"She didn't invite me. And it was only a couple of times, anyway."

"So you're a paragon of virtue. A semi-paragon, that is. Now we come to the nitty gritty. Did you talk about money? In particular, did she know you have a nice little nest egg tucked away?"

"Nope. I may have been a sucker, but I'm not a complete idiot. I just said I was a retired plumber. I didn't say I owned the business or that I had any other investments."

"Good." Zukie poured another cup of coffee and thought. The idea hit her so suddenly she almost jumped.

"What is it?" Lou asked.

"Your car. Maybe she really did leave her glasses there, which would be great, but even if she didn't, her fingerprints and DNA must be all over it. Jim could have forensics take a sample and see if she's who she says she is."

"They won't do that without a good reason, Zukie. Nobody got murdered in my car, did they?"

Zukie was already reaching for the telephone. Lou slammed his hand down over hers, making her wince.

"What was that for? He'll probably say no, anyway."

"Because I'd rather not have anyone else knowing about this. Let it drop."

Zukie stared at him for a minute. Then she said, "All right, Lou, have it your way. But if anything else happens – and I mean *anything* – I'm going straight to the cops. *Capisc'*?"

"Yeah."

"Can I look in your car and see if her glasses are there?"

"If it'll shut you up."

Zukie ignored that comment, took the keys and went out to Lou's car. She unlocked it and leaned into the passenger's side, looking for not only the glasses but anything else of interest. There was nothing on the seat, but in the glove compartment was a glasses case.

Zukie raised her eyebrows and wrapped a tissue around the case, lifting it out carefully, and opened the lid, revealing a pair of glasses too small to fit a man's face.

She checked the rest of the glove compartment, bent over to look under the seat and slid her hand down the crack between the seat and the back.

Nothing else came to light and so she locked the car again and

took the glasses case back into the house.
"Recognize these?" she asked Lou.

Chapter 4

"Yeah, I think they're Shirley's," Lou said. "She didn't wear them very often, just to read stuff."

"OK. That's fine. I'll put them in a safe place. I don't think you really want to return them to her and the cops might need them."

Lou rolled his eyes at the ceiling, but didn't argue. Zukie wrapped the case in a couple of paper towels and placed it in the drawer where she kept a collection of miscellaneous objects.

"We'll hang onto them just in case," she said, closing the drawer. "I'd like to think this is the end of the whole thing, but I have a feeling it isn't."

THE NEXT couple of days were nerve-wracking, at least to Zukie. Lou didn't seem concerned that he might have been the target of a homicidal motorist, but Zukie wasn't as blasé. In her opinion, it was a failed attempt at murder and that meant a second one might be made. The question, of course, was why, and she had no notion whatsoever what it might be.

So she followed Lou around on his daily outings until on the third day, he finally turned on her and snarled, "For God's sake, Zukie, you're getting to be a real pain in the ass. Leave me alone."

"Not yet. Not until I know what's happening."

"I'll be fine. Shove off."

They were in Tino's coffee shop, and Zukie was keeping her voice down with an effort. She and Lou knew most of the regulars, and when she'd seen him go inside, she supposed he would have been safe enough there, since they would have come to his aid if necessary. But they didn't need to know why she was sticking to him like used chewing gum to a shoe, and besides, Tino's pastries were calling to her.

Lou had settled himself at a table with his coffee, a glazed doughnut and the newspaper, only to look up and see his cousin sitting down on the other side of the table.

"I have every right to come in here and have a cappuccino if I want to," she said. "The pastries are pretty good, too."

She demonstrated by taking a bite of the cinnamon roll she was holding. Lou groaned and glared into his coffee cup.

Zukie had finished the cinnamon roll and half her cappuccino when Dave Iaducci, Lou's normal bowling partner, came through the door. He spotted them and came over to their table.

"Hi, Lou, Zukie."

"Hi, Dave," Zukie said cheerfully. "How you doing?"

"OK. How about you, Lou?"

Lou looked startled. "I'm fine. Why?"

"I thought you might be a little down."

Zukie immediately pounced on this, disregarding Lou's silent but eloquent plea for her to keep her mouth shut and mind her own business.

"Why would he be?"

Dave was flustered, and clearly didn't want to speak in front of her, but Zukie figured he shouldn't have made the comment if he didn't want it queried.

"I guess you split up with Shirley," he said finally.

"Yeah."

"How did you know that?" Zukie asked.

"Because I saw her in the Plane View yesterday on her own, looking real miserable."

"Good," Lou said.

Dave grinned. "Had a blow up, did you?"

"Something like that. It's no big deal."

"OK, I'll shut up. Glad you're all right."

"Sure. I'm fine. See you, Dave."

"DON'T THINK you're totally off the hook," Zukie warned Lou, when they had finished their coffee and withdrawn to the parking lot to consult. "I mean, it looks like she might be sitting there hoping you'll drop in. She probably knows you guys go there after bowling sometimes."

"Zukie, I don't think I'm so irresistible that she's going to be hanging around waiting for me to turn up, especially if I've got Dave and Neal with me."

"You're not that bad, Lou. In the right light, almost good-looking. But she can't expect you to be too excited about her after she set you up like that." A thought hit her. "Or maybe she thinks that guy really did run over you. Either way, you're not going to get back with her, are you?"

"As if."

"I'm glad to hear you say that. You know, Lou, I wouldn't stand in your way if you were really in love with somebody, but not someone like Shirley. I wouldn't trust her an inch."

"Very touching," Lou said. "Now, are you still going to follow me all over town, or go off and mind your own business?"

"Well, I feel a little better about it now, so if you promise to be careful, I'll leave you alone. I might go see Carol."

"Fine. I'll be at Lynn's if you need me."

"With your cell on?"

"If you insist."

They got in their respective cars are drove off in opposite directions. However, Zukie did not go very far. She drove a few blocks and then pulled over and took out her cell phone.

"Hey, Ange," she said. "Got a news flash for you."

"What's that?"

"Shirley's hanging around the Plane View. It looks like maybe she's hoping Lou will turn up."

Zukie had given her sister an abbreviated account of the mall incident the day it happened, had threatened Angela with dire consequences if she passed a word of it on, and had advanced the theory that Shirley had suddenly lost much of her charm where Lou was concerned. Angela had agreed that the odds were against the romance being resumed.

"I don't think that will fly, will it?" Angela said. "At least Lou is out of it now."

"I sure hope so. Anyway, I'd thought you'd like to know. I'm off to see Carol and Joe now."

"Say hi for me."

"OK. Talk to you later."

She put the phone away and started the engine.

CAROL AND Jim lived in a small wooden house in the heart of Georgetown, a neighborhood nestled more or less at the foot of Zukie's own Beacon Hill neighborhood and wedged up against the huge Boeing plant and adjoining airport. The area had a long history of welcoming immigrants and hard-working blue-collar families, but was currently undergoing gentrification, a term Zukie took to mean that normal people on average salaries could soon forget about buying a house there.

Fortunately, Jim Lanigan had purchased his house before the influx started, and he and Carol were happily settled there. Zukie looked at the house with satisfaction, envisioning Joe playing on a swing set in the back yard when he was a little older or riding a bike down the sidewalk.

She knocked on the front door, hoping she wasn't interrupting his naptime, although first-hand experience had shown Joe could sleep through anything short of a major earthquake. More likely, she'd be interrupting Carol in the middle of a phone call to one of her accountancy clients. She waited.

Eventually Carol answered the door, and since she wasn't

scowling, Zukie figured she was safe.

"Hi, sweetie. I was in the neighborhood and thought I'd drop by for a few minutes."

Carol looked skeptical, as well she might, but held the door open.

"Come on in. Do you want a cup of coffee?"

"Thanks." Zukie reflected that she had trained her daughter properly in at least one aspect. No one spent more than a minute inside Zukie's house without being offered at least a coffee, preferably accompanied by a piece of cake or some cookies.

Joe was in his playpen and gurgled happily on seeing her.

"Hey there, little guy." Zukie went over and lifted him out. "You been helping Mommy with her work?"

"He's actually been asleep most of the morning," Carol said from the kitchen. "If he'd sleep like that at night I'd be ecstatic, but no, he's a night owl like his dad."

"He'll get better," Zukie said, tickling his tummy. "You used to wake up at about three in the morning and wouldn't go back to sleep. Guess you thought you'd miss something."

"No wonder I'm an only child."

"Not *that*," Zukie said, mildly irritated. "But since you've brought the subject up, I have a piece of news for you."

"I can't imagine what piece of news would follow that," Carol said. She brought two cups of coffee and a small plate of cookies – store-bought, Zukie was sorry to see – and put them on the coffee table.

"It's about Lou."

"Oh, dear."

"Hush up and listen." Zukie shifted Joe to a secure position and held up a finger. "One, I found out where he was sneaking off to. He had a girlfriend."

A smile crept across Carol's face, which annoyed Zukie.

"What's so funny?"

"That's not illegal, Mom," she said. "He probably didn't want to listen to you lecture him on how she wasn't good enough for him."

"She wasn't." She held up another finger. "And now they've broken up."

"OK. Did you have anything to do with that?"

"No." A third finger. "He broke it off because on Friday, she tried to have someone run him over."

SHE WAS pleased to see this statement had an impact on Carol, who set her cup down and said, "You're joking."

"I'm not."

"Is Lou all right?"

"A little bruised, that's all. And he ruined a pair of pants and maybe his jacket as well."

"Did you report it to the police?"

"He wouldn't let me."

Carol knew her mother well enough to know nothing would stop Zukie from doing something if she really wanted to.

"Does he have any idea who the driver was?"

"No, 'cause I guess it all happened so quick, and of course he wasn't expecting it."

Zukie gave Carol a brief summary of the events at the mall and subsequent activity, ending up with, "So Dave saw her at the Plane View, sitting there all depressed. That's either 'cause she missed her chance to get her hands on his bank account or because she thinks he's dead and she's feeling kind of guilty, the *strega*."

"I'd go with number one," Carol said. "Partly because if she hangs around long enough she'll find out that Lou is alive and kicking. But why would she want him dead? It's not like he made a will leaving everything to her or an insurance policy with her as the beneficiary. At least I'd hope he didn't."

"No, of course he didn't. He's left everything to be split between Lynn and Vicki. The same with his life insurance. He told me."

"He wasn't planning to marry this Shirley, was he?"

"Not that I know of. He'd only known her a short time."

"So maybe it *was* a coincidence."

"Good grief, Carol, and you're a police detective's wife. It can't be just a coincidence and I'm not letting it rest until I find out what's going on. Whether Lou wants me to or not."

"Lucky Lou. Do you want another cup of coffee?"

"Sure. Thanks."

Carol took her cup and went into the kitchen. When she returned with the refilled cup, she said, "Why didn't Lou report it to the police?"

"I told you; I tried to get him to call up but he wouldn't. Too embarrassed, probably. And he wasn't seriously hurt."

Carol pondered this. Although married to a police detective, she fully understood the genetic reluctance to involve the police in private matters. In America as in the Old Country, Italians settled things behind the scenes, involving the law only when absolutely necessary.

Zukie drank her coffee, evading Joe, who was trying to grab the cup. Finally she said, "I wouldn't have mentioned it at all if I thought it was completely over. But if Shirley's hanging around hoping to reconnect with Lou or maybe even try this with someone else, well, I think I should keep an eye on things."

"You always do."

"Damn it, Carol, Lou's family."

"And he's perfectly capable of looking after himself."

"Oh, don't be silly. Men don't have any common sense in situations like this. Their brains are all in their …"

She stopped and looked guiltily at Joe, who gave her a gummy smile. It was depressing to think that this sweet little brown-eyed baby would grow up to be as clueless as most men where human relationships were concerned. Zukie patted his head.

"So what are you suggesting?" Carol asked. "The police can't stake out the Plane View parking lot waiting to see if this Shirley catches another victim."

"No, of course not. You aren't listening. I'm going to keep an eye on Lou until the whole thing blows over, that is, until she either gets tired of waiting around or finds someone else. She's not bad-looking, so that shouldn't be a problem."

"I can't think he's going to be too happy about that."

"Of course not, but he won't know. I told him I wouldn't be watching, so he won't be expecting me to. And I won't be obvious about it."

Carol opened her mouth, then shut it. She was willing to concede that her mother had her good points, but subtlety wasn't one of them. Her idea of a surreptitious stake-out would probably be to hide in a rhododendron bush with a pair of binoculars, or follow on the bumper of Lou's car wherever he might be going. Carol sighed.

"Well, it's up to you, Mom," she said. "Just don't complain when Lou loses it completely."

"I won't. He won't. But listen, sweetie."

"What?"

"It probably wouldn't hurt if you just kind of casually mentioned to Jim what I've told you."

SATISFIED that she had done all she could in the short term, Zukie gave Joe a final kiss and a tickle, thanked Carol for the coffee and headed back to her own house. She was relieved to see Lou's Buick parked in the driveway, proving that he had managed to get himself home safely after visiting his daughter.

She was even more relieved to see him sitting in the living room, reading the newspaper. She had always found that if you were going to say something that was apt to cause an argument, it was best to start at ground zero, so to speak, rather than confront someone who was already mad at you.

She shut the door behind her and Lou put the paper down.

"Did you tell Jim to get the cops to put a tail on me?"

Zukie's visions of a calm, rational discussion disintegrated before her eyes.

"*What?*"

Lou repeated his question. Zukie stared at him.

"No, of course not. I haven't seen or talked to Jim in, oh, almost a week."

"You sure about that?"

"Yes, I'm sure. What the heck are you talking about, Lou?"

"There's been a car following me around. I've seen it two or three times. An unmarked cop car. You remember Jim told us how to spot one?"

Zukie remembered. One evening after too many glasses of wine, Lanigan had been lulled into talking shop and Zukie had picked up several useful – to her way of thinking – tips for helping the police. Lanigan had been appalled to realize later that she had been taking copious mental notes from what he thought was a casual conversation, but he couldn't erase her memory and had sworn her to silence, especially where his boss was concerned. Over the last two years, Detective Lee Vance had racked up enough reasons to mistrust Zukie without adding another one.

"So when did this happen?" she asked.

"Today. I saw them when I left Tino's and again after I left Lynn's house. I don't think they were there before, or at least I didn't notice them before that. Zukie, you swear you had nothing to do with it?"

"Absolutely nothing, Lou. Cross my heart."

"Then what the heck …"

"Well, there's only two things I can think of."

"You amaze me. I thought there'd be at least a dozen."

Zukie ignored the dig. "One, they think you're up to something. Don't ask me what. Two, they're keeping an eye on you, trying to protect you from something. Don't ask me what that would be, either. But either way, Lou, you can bet your bottom dollar it has something to do with Shirley."

Chapter 5

Lou didn't answer immediately. Zukie hung her jacket up and sat down in an armchair facing him.

"I think you should have told the police about the incident at the mall."

"Sounds to me like they might already know. That's why I thought you were involved."

"Well, I'm not, but I admit I feel better now."

"Because I've got cops on my tail?" Lou's shaggy gray eyebrows nearly met his hairline as he lifted them in surprise.

"Sort of."

"Heaven help us. Or me, anyway."

He got up and stomped off in the direction of the kitchen. Zukie stayed where she was, staring at the brick fireplace as if it might hold a clue to the mystery. The faces in two wedding photographs – one of herself and Eddie and a newer one of Carol and Jim – stared back at her.

The sight of Jim Lanigan reminded her that he might be a source of information if Lou's observation was correct. Although she had no idea why the police might be following Lou around, she had been telling the truth about feeling he was a little safer now.

And she had certainly been telling the truth about believing Shirley was somehow involved.

Eventually she got up and followed Lou through the arch into the kitchen. He was filling the coffeemaker, a move Zukie approved of, since it looked like some serious thinking would be needed and her brain always worked better when fuelled by caffeine.

When it was bubbling away she said, "These cops didn't actually say anything to you, did they?"

"Nope. Just followed me."

"You sure you didn't imagine it?"

"No. OK, they weren't being obvious. I wouldn't have noticed anything if Jim hadn't told us what to look for. And they were trying a little too hard to pretend they weren't looking at me."

"How weird."

"You're telling me."

"And you haven't done anything to get cops on your tail?"

Lou just glared. Zukie supposed that was justified; he was a law-abiding retired plumber, not someone who engaged in any kind of illegal or even semi-legal activities. Setting off fireworks inside the city limits on the Fourth of July was about as nefarious an action as he ever took part in. And since that was a silly law and she liked fireworks, Zukie wholeheartedly approved of his breaking it.

"You don't imagine I could do anything illegal living here with you, anyway, do you?" Lou said. "You could give the FBI lessons in surveillance techniques."

Zukie correctly deduced the question was rhetorical, but she felt obliged to point out a flaw.

"You managed to sneak off to meet Shirley for heaven knows how long without me finding out. Even though everyone else seemed to know about it."

"It was only two or three weeks. I would have told you."

"When?"

Lou glared again but not as fiercely. In fact, Zukie could have sworn he actually blushed.

"Zukie, it wasn't serious. She was just someone to have a little fun with. Good company. You know what I mean. I never expected it to last very long. For one thing, she was a lot classier than me."

Zukie sniffed. She knew perfectly well what Lou was too embarrassed to say, and she wasn't going to help him out. If he felt guilty, he could take that up with Father Martin. But there was a more serious matter to be dealt with.

"Lou, what do you know about Shirley? Her background, I mean. If the police are involved, there must be something, and you're right, you haven't done anything, so it must have something to do with her."

Lou poured a cup of coffee, added milk and sugar and stirred it. Zukie correctly deduced this was to give him time to corral his thoughts and did the same, sitting down across the kitchen table from him. He poured a second cup for her, and when she figured he'd had long enough to think, she gave him a verbal nudge.

"Well?"

"I only know what she told me, and I already told you most of that. I'm a trusting soul; I don't run everything through the Angela gossip machine like you do. So what I'm saying is …"

"She could have fed you a complete crock and you'd have believed her. Jeez, Lou."

"Belt up. Don't you want to know what she said?"

"Course I do. Everything. Shoot."

"OK. Like I said, I met her in the parking lot between the Plane View and the bowling alley. She'd been at that little convenience store by the restaurant and couldn't get her car started."

"What kind of car?" Zukie asked.

"One with a dead battery."

"No, you idiot, what make? A beat-up wreck or a classy sports car or what?"

"Just an ordinary sedan."

"Not a black Ford?"

Lou blinked at her before he made the connection. "No. Not even close. Hers is silver and a different make and model. A Chevy."

"OK. Go on."

"So I jump-started her car, she thanked me and we got to talking. No big deal."

"I'm not interested in your smooth technique with women, Lou. What did she tell you about herself?"

"Not much, to be honest," Lou said, his eyebrows knitting together as he thought. "She said she was divorced and had just moved to this area and didn't know many people."

Zukie pantomimed playing a violin. "Poor thing. All alone in the big city. Where did she say she lived?"

"She didn't. Not exactly, anyway, but she did mention Georgetown."

"Or where she came from?"

"No."

Zukie felt like grabbing something and beating Lou over the head. Failure to supply details like these would have set off alarm bells in any woman of sound mind, but like most men, he had simply accepted it.

"So how did you meet up? It sounds like you didn't pick her up at her house and I know she didn't come here."

"We usually agreed to meet somewhere, like the mall."

"Or a motel. How classy."

"Shut it, Zuke. I didn't ask you for a lecture on morals."

Zukie let that one slide by, figuring he could go to confession if his conscience bothered him too much.

"OK. Did she seem to know much about Beacon Hill, or Georgetown, for that matter? Let's be honest – this end of town's not the first place a divorcee with a reasonable amount of money would want to live."

"How do you know she has a reasonable amount of money?"

Zukie sighed. "Her clothes. Her hair. Her manicure. So did she know her way around here?"

"I really couldn't say."

"So she may have been lying about being new to the area or even new to Seattle. What about the ex-hubby? She say anything about him?"

"One time she called him Mike, I think but that's about all. Why would I care?"

Zukie drained her coffee cup before answering.

"Lou, she might still be married. She might never have been married at all. Or she might be a widow. She might have killed her husband."

"Oh, good grief. Look, I didn't ask to see the divorce decree. She said she was divorced, so I took her word for it."

It was worrying that he took the word of a total stranger when he never trusted his own cousin. Zukie shook her head and said, "So what did you talk about with her?"

"Sports. She likes baseball. Food. She likes to cook."

"Hmph."

"I'm sure she's not as good as you, Zuke, so no need to get all huffy. I never ate anything she cooked, so I don't know how good she might be."

"Probably just as well. Italian food?"

"Could be. She was asking where she could get certain stuff, and I suggested Colonna's. That's why we were there when you charged in with your guns blazing."

Zukie ignored the inaccurate description of her entrance and considered. "So she's not from around here, 'cause if she was, she'd already know about Colonna's and I probably would have seen her before."

"Yeah, probably. Good point."

"And you said before she told you she'd quit her job. She seems too young to be retired, so what was she living on? Thin air? Divorce settlement? Gullible men?"

"Again – I don't know. She never asked me for any money and I didn't give her any or promise her any, so you can stop that before you start."

"Not even a suggestion?"

"Nope."

Zukie could see that Lou was doing his best, but hadn't bothered to confirm what she considered to be the most basic details about the woman. And he certainly hadn't learned anything that shed a light on why a speeding car in a parking garage had nearly deprived her of her housemate. She had no intention of dropping the subject, so she would have to tackle it another way.

"OK, flip it around. What did you tell her about yourself? You can't have discussed the Mariners and spaghetti sauce the whole time."

"I said I was retired, widowed and have two daughters."

"Anything else?"

"Nothing about you, if that's what you're hinting. You're just my landlady."

Zukie's hand closed around the salt shaker as she contemplated letting it fly at Lou's head. Instead, she got a grip on herself and said, "You didn't say where you lived? The address or the street, I mean, not that you live in my house."

"I said I lived up by Cleveland High School. That's all."

"And did she seem to know where that was?"

"Not really. Of course, if she'd just moved here, she wouldn't."

That was a relief, since Zukie didn't want a woman maddened by rejection to turn up on the doorstep, even if she'd jump-started the rejection with an attempted murder. She had a feeling Lou didn't have much else to contribute and the stubborn expression on his face told her that even if he did, he wasn't going to share it. There were other ways of uncovering information.

"OK, Lou, if you don't know anything else about her, then you don't."

"You're going to get Angela snooping around, aren't you?"

Zukie twitched at this evidence of mind-reading. "You have to admit she's good at it."

"A little too good, if you ask me. Don't stir up any dust, Zukie. It's over."

"Except for the cops on your tail."

"Maybe I imagined that."

"I don't think so. Not if you saw them more than once."

A gloomy silence descended over the kitchen, broken finally by Lou saying, "OK, I guess I blew it. All I wanted was a little female company – aside from you, that is – and got myself involved in something weird. The question is what, if anything, I can do about it now. Maybe I should go up to the Plane View after all and have it out with her."

It was tempting, but Zukie could see several drawbacks, one of which was that she would insist on coming along to keep Lou from doing anything stupid and he would insist that she mind her own damn business and stay home.

"No, it's probably better just to make a clean break and hope she loses interest," she said.

"How about the cops?"

"Well, if nothing happens, they'll lose interest, too, I guess."

"Fine, then that's what I'll do. Nothing."

"Sounds like a plan. You want to watch a DVD? Or, I know what, let's go to the casino. That's far enough away that if the cops are really following you, we'll spot them."

Lou knew perfectly well that this was not a totally disinterested suggestion, since Zukie loved to visit the nearest tribal casino. She was watching him with narrowed eyes and he gave in.

"Sure, why not? It's better than sitting here being grilled by you or waiting for someone to drive a car through the living room window."

"They better not," Zukie said, "Or a dead battery will be the least of her problems."

IT WAS unthinkable that Zukie would go to the casino wearing her usual jeans and sweatshirt, even though that was what most people did. She knew she would never swan through the doors of a Monte Carlo casino or even a Las Vegas establishment, so she liked to pretend the local casino was far more exotic than it was. And Lou had become resigned to the fact that he was cast in the James Bond role, although he refused to dress the part.

So Zukie went to change into a smarter pair of pants and a matching sweater, and swapped her worn track shoes for boots. There wasn't much to be done about her hair, but she did add a swipe of lipstick for a touch of glamour.

"You look fine," Lou said, anticipating the usual question. "Come on, let's hit the road."

Neither of them said much on the way to the casino. Zukie was lost in contemplation of both Shirley and the casino's buffet table, and whatever Lou was thinking, he wasn't about to share it. Occasionally she surfaced long enough to glance in the side mirror to see if anything resembling an unmarked police car was following them, but if it was, its driver was adroit enough not be noticed.

Lou pulled into the casino parking lot and Zukie put a hand on his arm to keep him in the car, glancing around to see if anyone had followed them in. The only other car which had just entered had disgorged four middle-aged women, who, on the face of it, were unlikely to be undercover police officers. They sat in the car for a full minute, waiting, but no one else appeared.

"Looks like the coast is clear," she said, opening her door.

"Maybe they've lost interest, like you said," Lou said. "I don't know what that was all about anyway."

They went through the casino doors and Zukie faced her usual dilemma – whether to stuff her face first at the buffet or have a turn at the slot machines and then either celebrate or console herself in the restaurant. Lou watched her with amusement.

"Better have lunch first," he advised. "Then if we lose our pensions, at least we won't need to buy food for a while."

"Good thinking." Zukie led the way to the restaurant area, collected a plate and moved along the buffet, filling it with barbecued chicken wings, sliced ham, potato salad and coleslaw. Feeling virtuous, she added a few cherry tomatoes and a wedge of cantaloupe.

"No dessert?" Lou asked her.

"Maybe later. If I win."

"Fine. I'll roll you back in here so you can have some blueberry pie and ice cream."

Zukie winced. She absolutely loved blueberry pie and made it herself when blueberries were in season. But she remembered the number that had blinked up at her from the bathroom scales that morning and decided pie abstinence might not be a bad thing. On the other hand, perhaps the scales were faulty.

"We'll see," she said.

They sat down at a table and Zukie dug into her loaded plate, still looking around occasionally to see if anyone seemed interested in them. She wasn't sure she'd be able to recognize a plainclothes police officer if it was someone she didn't know personally, but she thought she could recognize if someone was taking an unnatural interest in two middle-aged casino customers with nothing special to distinguish them.

When they'd finished eating, and Zukie had reluctantly decided to skip dessert, they went out onto the floor. She stationed herself in front of one of her favorite machines and Lou wandered off to try his luck on another row.

For a while, she forgot all about Lou's abortive romance and the possibility that he had involved himself in something sinister. The world had narrowed to the rows of symbols on the screen in front of her and she let out a muted whoop of triumph when she saw them line up and the lights flashed.

Zukie prided herself on knowing to quit when she was ahead, so she collected her winning ticket and started for the cashier. Lou, spotting her and recognizing the signs, shoved a five-dollar bill into the slot and watched it disappear without giving him anything lucrative in return. By the time he reached Zukie, she was stuffing her winnings into her purse and zipping her coat up, ready to leave.

"That was a waste of time," he said, as they walked back to the car.

"Speak for yourself. I won twenty bucks."

"Bet that nearly broke the bank. No I mean, because we didn't spot any cop cars after me."

"Well, no. That's not a bad thing, though, is it?"

It might have been the fact that she'd won some money or the fact that Lou seemed to have lost his police escort, but Zukie felt much more relaxed as they drove back on the freeway. The feeling of well-being lasted until they were nearly at the exit to Beacon Hill and Zukie's cell phone rang.

She glanced at the caller identification and said, "Hi, Shelly. What's up?"

"Where are you, Zukie?"

"On I-5, heading back to the house. We've been out at the casino. Why?"

Zukie thought she heard Shelly lower her voice, as if she were afraid of being overheard. That was unnerving, but nothing compared to what she heard next.

"Zukie, there's an unmarked police car parked in front of your house."

"How do you know it's a police car?"

"Because that detective, Vance, is in it, along with a woman cop. He doesn't look very happy."

"He never does."

"No, seriously. He keeps looking at the house and then talking on his cell. So I don't think it's a social call."

"It wouldn't be. He's not social. OK, we'll be there shortly, and find out what it's about. Thanks, Shelly."

"What was that?" Lou asked, swinging onto the exit ramp.

"Vance is sitting in a police car front of the house, and there's another cop there as well."

Lou braked so suddenly that Zukie half expected to be smothered by an inflated air bag. She jerked back in her seat and the driver of the car behind them honked furiously.

"Vance? As in Homicide Detective Lee Vance?"

"Yes. Oh, my God." Zukie gulped, as the possibilities unfolded in front of her. "You don't think that …."

"One way to find out," Lou said grimly. He accelerated again and drove the next few blocks in silence.

Neither of them spoke until they were pulling into the

driveway, when Lou said, "Watch what you say, Zukie."

"Let's see what they say first," she replied, displaying what Lou considered a rare burst of common sense.

Vance was out of the car and waiting as they climbed out.

"Hi there," Zukie said.

Vance nodded. "Mrs Merlino. Mr Romano."

"Can we help you with something?" Lou asked.

"I don't know yet," Vance said. "But it's possible that you in particular, Mr Romano, can provide me with some information."

"About what?"

"A woman named Shirley Minghella."

"Why?" Zukie asked, before she could stop herself.

"Because we understand Mr Romano was a friend of hers. And because Shirley Minghella is dead."

Chapter 6

Zukie felt her knees wobble and she clutched the fender of Lou's car to keep from staggering. Lou himself looked as though he'd been hit over the head with a blunt instrument. He stared silently at Vance as if hoping his announcement was some kind of extremely tasteless joke.

"Dead?" Zukie asked. "Where? When? How?"

"Let's discuss this inside the house, shall we?" Vance suggested. He beckoned to the woman who had gotten out of the passenger seat. "This is Detective Corinne Holt. She'll be working with me on this." Holt brought up the rear as Zukie unlocked the door and the four of them went inside.

"What happened to Shirley?" Lou asked. He sat down heavily on the sofa and Zukie perched beside him, trying to remember the CPR instructions she'd once read, in case he collapsed.

The two detectives took the armchairs and Vance said, "First things first. I'm correct in thinking you knew Ms Minghella quite well?"

"I suppose you'd say so. Yes, I did."

Vance produced a notebook and ballpoint pen. Zukie thought he really should be using a more technologically advanced method of taking notes, but decided it wasn't the time to comment. She shot a glance at Lou, who was paler than usual, but outwardly calm enough.

"Can you tell me when was the last time you saw her?"

"About three or four days ago."

"Where was that?"

"At the mall."

Zukie cringed, hoping the whole story of the incident in the parking garage wouldn't come out, or if it did, that Vance wouldn't be too angry that it hadn't been reported. It wasn't her fault, she thought virtuously. She had tried to persuade Lou but he'd been too stubborn.

"And you haven't seen her since then?"

"No, because we split up."

Zukie dared to breathe again.

"Can you tell us what happened to her?" she asked, as politely as she could manage.

"No," Vance said. "Questions first, then answers."

"Although I guess since you're here from Homicide, she must have been murdered. Either of you want some coffee?"

The question just popped out, since offering food and drink was Zukie's solution to most of life's problems.

"No, thank you," Vance said, and Holt shook her head. "Mr Romano, how long had you known Ms Minghella before your relationship ended?"

"Not that long. A month or so. Maybe a little longer."

"A short relationship, then."

"Yeah."

"Were you on intimate terms with her?"

Lou glared, but kept himself from snarling a response. Zukie admired him for that, because under the circumstances, she probably would have snapped back that it was none of Vance's business.

"You could call it that. Why?"

"Did she speak to you at all about her background – where she was from, what sort of work she'd done, anything like that?"

"Not much. She said she was divorced and new to Seattle. That's about all."

Vance made a couple of notes. "She said she was divorced. Did she say anything about her former husband?"

"Not much. I think she called him Mike."

"Nothing about what kind of business he was in?"

"No."

Zukie was twitching restlessly. Vance threw her a look and said, "You'll get your chance in a minute, Mrs Merlino."

"Chance for what?"

"To talk."

Zukie bristled at that, considering it was her house and her second cousin being grilled about the death of a woman he should never have been mixed up with in the first place. Detective Holt gave her what might have been intended as a reassuring smile.

"Do you know where she was living?" Vance asked Lou.

"No. She mentioned Georgetown, but I don't know any more than that."

Zukie had to admit Lou's answers probably sounded fishy to Vance, but then the detective wasn't living in a neighborhood where everybody minded everybody else's business and would be happy to spread the news that Lou Romano was seeing a good-looking divorcee whom nobody knew anything about. As annoyed as she had been with him, she could understand why he'd wanted to keep quiet about the relationship.

"So you never went to her home."

"No."

Vance tapped his pen in what could have been frustration. He was a stern-faced man in his forties, and his acquaintance with the two of them – Zukie in particular – had been problematic from the start. It didn't look like improving any time soon.

"And in fact you know very little about her."

"I suppose so."

"Did she ever leave anything with you for safekeeping?"

Zukie's eyebrows shot up at the question and she looked at Lou. He was frowning, indicating he was as puzzled as she was.

"No. What sort of thing?"

"Unfortunately, I don't know."

Zukie cleared her throat and said, "How about her glasses, Lou?"

"Glasses?" Holt asked.

"She left them in my car," Lou said, neatly sidestepping the issue of the possible murder attempt.

"And do you still have them?"

"Yes."

"Why didn't you return them to her when you split up?"

Zukie and Lou looked at each other. Zukie felt she was going to be shouted at for mentioning the glasses as soon as the police officers were out the door, which wasn't really fair, considering they'd landed in the middle of a homicide investigation and the information could be helpful. She nodded encouragingly at Lou, to get him to spill the details.

"It's a long story," Lou said, giving in.

"I've got plenty of time," Vance said. "Let's hear it."

IT WAS nearly a half an hour later before Lou had recounted the entire episode at the mall, long enough for even Vance to break down and accept a cup of coffee from Zukie. He wrote down every detail Lou could remember, and Zukie contributed her share, even though she suspected Vance thought she was making them up.

"And you still have her glasses?" Holt asked.

"Yep," Zukie said. "I saved them, just in case you needed to get DNA or something off them."

"Why?" Vance asked.

"Why what?"

"Why did you think we might need to do that?"

"For Pete's sake," Zukie said, forgetting her vow to be polite. "It looked like she set Lou up to be run over. That's not a nice, friendly thing to do, so I thought she might be some kind of crook. In which case, you guys might like to know more about her. She might not even be using her real name."

"What makes you say that?"

Zukie was momentarily speechless. It seemed obvious to her that if someone was a potential criminal, she might use a false name, especially when targeting a retired plumber for some dishonest reason. She decided to skip that explanation and go on to the logical deduction.

"So she *was* using a false name?"

"We didn't say she was," Holt said. "Nor do we, at this point, consider her a criminal."

Zukie remembered Angela saying that the name Minghella rang a distant bell with her. Obviously the next job was to see what her sister could dredge out of her memory. There were few areas where Zukie would concede her talents were less than Angela's, but remembering details of neighborhood gossip over the decades was one of them.

"Can I see the glasses?" Vance asked.

"Sure." Zukie got up and went to the kitchen, where she took the carefully wrapped package from the drawer. She handed it to Vance, who removed the paper towels, donned a latex glove and opened the glasses case. He didn't touch the glasses themselves, just studied them for a minute, and then closed the case again.

"Thank you," he said to Zukie, who felt she might be forgiven by him, if not by Lou. "We'll take these back to the lab."

"Course if you already know who she is, they may not help," Zukie said.

"We know what identification she was carrying," Vance said. "Who she is might not be exactly the same thing."

"But what ..." Zukie sputtered to a halt, trying to read between the lines. "Why do you think she might not be who she said she was?"

"That's confidential information, I'm afraid."

"OK. So how'd you know she knew Lou?"

Zukie knew by the expression on Vance's face and the little gasp she heard from Detective Holt that this was not a welcome question. And yet it seemed obvious to her that it needed to be asked and answered.

"An item found on the body."

Zukie looked at Lou. "Did you give her anything, Lou?"

"No."

"So what was it?"

"Thank you for your help, Mr Romano," Vance said, ignoring both Zukie's question and the laser-like glare she was aiming in his direction. "I would say I was sorry for your loss, but considering the way your relationship with Ms Minghella ended, that might not be appropriate. If you think of anything else that might be useful, please contact me or Detective Holt."

He put the notebook away, stood up and started toward the door. Holt followed his lead.

"Just a second," Zukie said, unwilling to let them escape without wringing one last bit of information from them. "You never said how she died. Or where or when. So I guess you don't think Lou or me killed her, since you're not asking us for an alibi."

"No, I'm not."

"Course maybe you already know where we were at the time, whenever it was, since you've been following Lou around for a few days."

Vance had his hand on the doorknob. He removed it, turned to face her and said, "How on earth did you know that, Mrs Merlino?"

ZUKIE WAS unwilling to get Jim Lanigan into trouble, so she decided to try a combination of the truth and fibs, a technique that had held her in good stead most of her life.

"Lou thought he saw the same car – or at least the same kind of car – following him a few times in the last two or three days. Since he split up with Shirley, that is. OK, it might have been someone else or just coincidence, but the car was the kind of unmarked ones you guys use and the drivers looked like cops."

"Looked like cops," Vance repeated. "How so?"

Zukie floundered. "Well, kind of stern and official looking, but pretending like they weren't, you know what I mean?"

Vance looked as though he wanted to hit his head against the door. He said, "Very observant, Mrs Merlino, but hardly conclusive."

"Oh, for Pete's sake," Zukie said, feeling her good intentions rapidly unravelling. "You know me, don't you? And you know Lou, too, and so you know darn well neither of us would have killed this Shirley. And you've more or less admitted your guys were following Lou. So what the heck's going on?"

If ever a man had looked as though he were caught on the horns of a dilemma, it was Lee Vance. Zukie, of course, knew the reason. Vance was perfectly aware she was plugged in to the neighborhood gossip machine, had a shrewd – if somewhat chaotic – thought process, and had been helpful to him in solving previous cases.

And yet he never completely trusted her, thanks to her habit of almost literally diving into action before engaging her brain, and also because of her tendency to take a few vague hints and develop them into a theory only slightly related to hard facts backed up by evidence. She was often correct, something that she knew irked him even further.

So she said graciously, "If it's something top secret, you don't have to tell us. As long as you didn't consider either of us suspects. And if we can help at all, I'm sure you'll let us know, won't you?"

Vance must have sighed inwardly in relief, but his face remained impassive.

"Of course I will."

"And there's nothing else you can tell us?"

"Not at the moment. And don't try to grill Jim Lanigan, either."

"I wouldn't dream of it."

"As you so rightly noted, I know you, Mrs Merlino. So don't try it."

"OK."

They locked gazes for a second or two, and then Vance turned the doorknob.

"If there's anything you *need* to know, I'll be in touch. But since you're not family and her relationship with Mr Romano was over, I doubt that there will be anything."

"Guess that's about the best we can hope for," Zukie said, forcing a cheerful tone. "Good luck."

"Thank you," Holt said.

After the door had closed behind the two officers, Zukie and Lou looked at each other.

"This is seriously weird," Zukie said. "Why the heck did Vance come here to grill you about Shirley being murdered and then wouldn't even say when or where or how she died?"

"You expect me to answer that?"

"Not really. It's one of those rhetorical questions." Zukie had barely scraped through high school, thanks to her habit of ignoring any classwork she found boring, but her reading habits were wide-ranging and her vocabulary occasionally startled Lou.

"What kind's that?"

"Ones that don't have answers. You want some coffee, Lou?"

"I'd rather have a stiff drink, but yeah, coffee's fine."

Zukie put the coffeemaker on, her mind working furiously. When the coffee was ready, they sat on either side of the kitchen table and Zukie gazed into her cup.

"I don't know what's going on here," she said finally, "but if Vance didn't want me to get involved, he shouldn't have said anything. OK, maybe he thought you'd be able to tell him something useful, but he should know better than to dangle something like that in front of me and expect me to ignore it."

"Maybe he thought you'd have enough sense to stay out, although he should have known that wouldn't happen, either."

"I don't have much to go on, I admit, but I'm going to get to the bottom of this. I mean, we only have his word for it she's really dead."

"Why would he lie about something like that?"

"I don't know, but I think there's something really weird going on."

"Saints preserve us," Lou said.

IN THE precinct station, Vance faced Holt over a desk, much as Lou and Zukie were doing, minus the strong Italian coffee. Styrofoam cups of brown liquid from the vending machine made an unsatisfactory substitute.

"How the hell does she do it?" he said.

"Is that a rhetorical question?" Holt asked, unconsciously echoing Zukie.

"Probably. Who else would have saved the glasses Shirley left in Romano's car? Who else would have questioned whether she was using a false name? And noticed the unmarked car following him?"

"It was Romano who spotted that, from what I gathered, not Mrs Merlino. Do you think he's involved at all, sir?"

"I don't think so. If nothing else, his reaction when we told him she was dead. He turned white as a sheet. Besides, he has no criminal record whatsoever, and I've checked him out ten ways to Sunday. Respectable retired business owner, pillar of the community, church-goer, all-round good guy, except for a lamentable lapse in judgement in not only being related to Susanna Merlino but actually sharing a house with her."

"So why did Shirley get involved with him?" Holt asked, sipping her lukewarm coffee. "You wouldn't have expected that, would you?"

"Maybe another lapse in judgement. Maybe she just liked the guy and their relationship has nothing to do with anything else. Who knows, but I sure would like to find out, if only to rule him out."

"You won't find out from her, obviously."

"No." Vance drained his coffee. "I don't know how the hell she got that careless, but it's too late to do anything about it now."

Holt correctly judged she wasn't expected to comment.

"That was an idiotic thing to do, putting those plainclothes units on. I wish they'd cleared it with me first, because I would have deep-sixed the idea. Not only did Romano make them, but it just put him more on his guard. OK, he had a brief fling with her. That doesn't mean he's involved any deeper than that, unless someone finds some proof that he is."

"What did you make of the incident in the parking garage?" Holt asked. "That seemed out of character."

"Yes, a little too obvious. If Romano was really the target, why do something as ridiculous as sideswiping him? One shot would have been all they needed."

"Unless it was intended to draw her onto the scene, maybe when he didn't come back to the restaurant."

"Possibly." Vance lifted his cup again, discovered it was empty, and chewed a pen instead. "If so, it backfired. The only thing that happened as a result was that Romano decided he could live without her, and cut her off. Not that I blame him, under the circumstances."

"No. So where do we go from here, sir?"

"At the moment," Vance said, "I really don't know. Suggestions?"

Chapter 7

As usual, when she had a dilemma to deal with, Zukie turned to cooking. Lou was the unwitting beneficiary of this practice, and although he didn't know it yet, he was going to get a superb dinner that night because of that dilemma.

Lou himself had fled the scene, saying he didn't want to listen to her crackpot theories, so Zukie had a clear field, not that she had any real idea what to do with it. At the moment, very little of what Vance said made sense to her. She supposed she had to accept that Shirley was dead, although she would have liked some concrete proof of that. On the other hand, she had stumbled across a couple of murder victims in the past and hadn't enjoyed the experience.

So the first question was why anyone would want to murder a woman who seemed fairly ordinary, with no obvious enemies.

But you don't know that, she reminded herself. *In fact, you know hardly anything about Shirley Minghella, or whatever her name is. And neither does Lou.*

Zukie put some thin beef steaks to soak in an olive oil and balsamic vinegar marinade, crushing two cloves of garlic with the heel of her hand, and adding them to the mix. Smashing the cloves gave her a certain amount of satisfaction, as she imagined crushing some part of Vance's anatomy. She washed and dried her hands, shoved the pan into the fridge, and went to the telephone.

"Hey, Ange," she said when her sister answered. "I got a problem."

She pretended she didn't hear Angela sighing.

"What is it, Zuke?"

"You know that Shirley that Lou was seeing?"

"Yeah. What about her?"

"Detective Vance, Jim's boss, came by here a little while ago and told us she's been murdered."

There was dead silence on the other end of the phone, indicating Angela probably thought her older sister had finally lost her marbles.

"Did you hear me?" Zukie demanded.

"Course I heard you. You said Shirley's dead. Who killed her?"

"If I knew that, I wouldn't be calling you. He just asked Lou a load of questions, and Lou couldn't answer most of them. Like where Shirley was living, and so on, 'cause he never bothered to find out."

"Men," Angela said, covering all the bases with one word.

"I know. Anyway, the strangest thing he asked was whether she'd left anything with Lou for safekeeping. The only thing she left was her glasses, and she didn't really leave them because she sent him back to get them out of the car. And anyway, what would be worth 'safekeeping' about a pair of glasses?"

Angela worked her way through that and then said, "What happened to the glasses in the end?"

"Vance took them away."

"So maybe there was something special about them after all."

"I can't see what. The only thing would be to get DNA off them."

"And why would they need that?"

"I don't know, do I? The usual reason would be for identification – you know, to make sure she was who she said she was."

Angela didn't answer immediately. Finally she said, "So what's your problem? It sounds like the cops are investigating her death."

"The problem is that Lou is involved. They just might come

up with the hare-brained idea that he killed her."

"Why would he?"

"Shut up and listen, Ange. The cops were following him around for a day or so before she got killed. So it looks like they think he's done something."

"But if they were following him, they'd know he didn't kill her."

"They weren't following him twenty-four seven, you know."

"Well, I know you won't pay any attention to me," Angela said, stating an undeniable truth, "but I think you should stop worrying about it so much. I mean, Vance knows Lou. It's not like he's some guy he never met before and thinks might be connected to a crime."

Zukie had to admit that made a certain amount of sense, although it didn't do much toward easing her mind. Lou might be older than her and had demonstrated over the years he was perfectly capable of looking after himself, but she still felt responsible for his welfare. He was family, and that meant that if there was anything she could do to help him, she was obliged to do so. The police would undoubtedly disagree, but that was their problem.

She felt she shouldn't need to explain all this to Angela, so she said only, "I don't trust Vance."

"Why not?"

"Because he might decide to take the easy way out and arrest Lou without any evidence."

"I don't think they can do that, Zuke."

"No, not if I make sure it doesn't happen. So I need your help, Ange."

"Oh, my God. Doing what?"

"What you do best. Poke and pry."

"Thanks."

Zukie ignored this. "You said the name Minghella rang a bell with you. That's the name Shirley was using, even if it wasn't her real one. So I need you to dig back and come up with anything at all connected with that name. And if you can come up with a Mike or Mick or Michael Minghella, that would be even better."

"Who are they?"

"It's only one guy, Ange. Possibly her ex-husband."

"What does he have to do …"

"I don't know. I just want something to get my teeth into. So see if you can find me something. Anything."

VANCE LACKED a researcher like Angela, but he was just as eager to get his investigation under way. He had already sent the glasses Zukie had salvaged to the police laboratory to see if anything could be gleaned from them, and was now handing out assignments to his detectives.

"It's obvious that Shirley didn't tell Romano anything resembling the truth," he told them. "She said she was a divorcee, that she was new to Seattle and that she lived in Georgetown. We know that only the first one of those statements was true. I am guessing she just wanted to blow some smoke in case he tried to visit her at home, something like that.

"On the other hand, it's fairly obvious she didn't intend to be involved with him for long. That's not insulting Romano, just stating a fact. She was using him for something, and the most likely something is as a cover for her real activities."

His audience nodded solemnly.

"If she had realized he was connected to someone like Susanna Merlino, I'm sure she would have picked someone else, but we all make mistakes. Unfortunately, she can't do anything about it now, and much as I would like to lock Mrs Merlino away, I don't think she's involved in this except in a peripheral way."

He shot Jim Lanigan an almost apologetic glance.

"Sorry, Lanigan, but you know what she's like."

"All too well. But you have to admit she's been helpful on occasion."

"This won't be one of them, if I can possibly help it."

"I understand."

"Good." Vance looked around. "I don't know who Shirley was reporting to, so I don't know what kind of evidence, if any, she had been able to put together. I'll have to do some liaising first, and probably some bowing and scraping as well. Those guys think they're superior to those of us who just find out who killed somebody, and if we're lucky, even why they did it. So here's what we'll do …"

ZUKIE HAD decided to pull out all the stops for dinner, conveniently forgetting her vow at the casino to ease back on the calories. So while the steaks were marinating, she mixed up the batter for a pineapple upside down cake, justifying it to herself by reasoning that fruit was healthy and pineapples were undeniably fruit.

She melted brown sugar and butter in the cake pan, covered the mixture with canned pineapple chunks, then poured the batter over it all and popped it into the oven. While it was baking, she peeled potatoes to make the chunky fries that Lou liked, and when those were done, sliced zucchini to sauté along with some fresh mushrooms.

The scent of the cake baking brought Lou into the kitchen, a somewhat hang-dog but mulish expression on his face.

"Something smells good," he said.

"Pineapple upside down cake. I know you like that."

"If you're trying to bribe me with cake, I know you want something."

"Not necessarily, Lou."

"OK. Does that mean you're not going to nag me any more about Shirley?"

"Again, not necessarily. You couldn't have known what you were getting into."

"What exactly *have* I gotten into, Zuke?"

Zukie put the paring knife down, to lessen temptation.

"You're in the middle of a homicide investigation, Lou,

remember? If Vance didn't know you, you'd probably be top of the suspect hit parade."

"I'd broken up with her. You don't kill someone you've only been dating a few weeks, even if they were stalking you or something, and she wasn't."

"But you didn't exactly break up with her, did you? You just never came back from the parking garage. That's kind of inconclusive, you might say. Tell me, Lou, if that car hadn't side-swiped you, would you still be dating her?"

"I suppose so," Lou said, after a moment's thought. "What are you getting at?"

"I was just thinking that maybe someone was trying to deliberately split you up for some reason. Let's face it, if they were really trying to kill you, they would have shot you."

She said this so casually that Lou blinked, although he had to admit she was right. Trying to run over someone in a parking garage was a fairly haphazard form of attempted homicide.

"But how did they know I'd be there? I still think she set me up."

"I don't know."

"I'm glad to hear there's something you don't know. When's dinner?"

MELLOWED by tender steak, crisp fries, sautéed zucchini and mushrooms, followed by the pineapple upside down cake and coffee, Lou was in a better mood by the time he'd finished. Zukie was glad to observe this, since she had no intention of letting the matter drop.

She waited until Lou had washed the dishes and she had cleaned the stove top and counters, and then steered him into the living room.

"What's up?" he asked apprehensively. "I was going to watch TV."

"TV can wait. Tell me exactly what happened when you went back to the parking garage."

"Oh, my God, Zukie, not again. You said you weren't going to nag me about it anymore."

"No, I didn't. Something's missing."

"Yeah, your brains."

"*State' zitt*," Zukie said. Neither she nor Lou spoke Italian with any degree of fluency, but they knew some useful phrases, like being able to tell someone to shut up. She returned to the task at hand.

"Start with going to the restaurant for lunch. Which one were you at?"

Lou groaned, but realizing he wasn't going to be released until he'd been wrung dry, he sank into an armchair.

"That seafood one at the back of the mall. I can't remember the name."

"I know which one you mean. OK. Whose idea was it to go there?"

"Hers. She likes – liked – clam chowder."

"And you can see the parking garage entrance if you're sitting in the front of the restaurant, I bet. Were you?"

"Yes. You ever thought of applying for a job with the cops? Or maybe going to law school so you could go all Perry Mason and cross-examine witnesses? You got a knack for it, you know."

"Thanks." Zukie was flattered, even though she knew it had been meant as an insult. "Now, what happened next?"

Lou sighed. "The waitress came over and gave us each a menu. Shirley said she couldn't quite make it out and opened her purse to get her reading glasses. She couldn't find them and said she thought she remembered putting them in the glove compartment of my car, and would I mind getting them for her."

"Course you could have just read her the menu. Wonder what would have happened if you'd done that?"

They stared at each other and Lou said, "No idea. Maybe it really was a coincidence."

"Or something else would have happened at another time. So you, being a complete gentleman, went off to the garage to get her glasses. Anything else she said or did?"

Lou appeared to be thinking hard, so Zukie let him think.

"She said to take my jacket because it was cold outside. So I did."

Before Lou had finished the last three words, Zukie was off. She zipped through the kitchen and down the stairs to the basement, where her washing machine and dryer were located.

The jacket Lou had worn that day was still in the laundry basket, ripped sleeve and all, because he had another jacket to wear and if there was one thing Zukie hated more than ironing, it was mending. She'd just dropped it there when they returned from the mall, on the off chance the mending fairy would repair it and she wouldn't have to bother.

Carefully folding the jacket over her arm, she carried it back upstairs to where Lou was scratching his head and wondering, not for the first time, if his cousin had lost her mind. He looked somewhat relieved to see her returning with only a dirty, crumpled jacket.

"What are you doing with that?"

Zukie declined to answer such a silly question and spread the jacket out on the sofa, sleeves outstretched. She began running her fingers over the garment, inch by inch, and then deciding that would take too long, simply turned it inside out and shook it vigorously.

Something rolled out of a small inside pocket and landed on the sofa cushion. Zukie pounced, grabbing it before it disappeared down the crack between the seat and the back.

"What the heck is that?" Lou asked. "I never put anything in there. The only inside pocket I use is that bigger one, to put my phone in."

"So someone else did and I'll give you one guess who."

Zukie opened her hand and held the tiny object out for Lou to look at. He leaned over to examine it.

It was only an inch or so long, a tiny carved piece of what appeared to be ivory. It depicted a fish, its tail curved around to meet its mouth, and was so intricate that they could make out every scale. It was slightly worn, the creamy color darkened a little around the fish's mouth and fins.

"What is it?" Lou asked, frowning.

"It's one of those little Japanese carvings," Zukie said. "They're called *netsuke* and they used to use them kind of like toggles to hold things shut."

Lou just looked at her and she said, "I read an article about them somewhere."

That didn't surprise him. Zukie's reading material ranged from encyclopedias to the backs of cereal boxes and once she read something, she rarely forgot it, unless she did so deliberately.

"People collect them now," she continued, touching it with a fingertip. "Being as the Japanese use buttons and zippers and pockets like anyone else these days. Most of the *netsuke* are at least a hundred years old, sometimes older. So if they're old ones, and genuine, they're worth a pile of money. This one looks like it's made of ivory, like a lot of them were. And I suppose like anything that people collect, some are a lot rarer than others and worth more. Remember Frank Martinelli's coins?"

Lou would have preferred to forget the first homicide case Zukie had involved herself in, but he nodded.

"So what the hell is a rare Japanese antique toggle thing doing in my jacket pocket?"

"Shirley put it there, probably when you took your jacket off in the restaurant. Could she have done that?"

"I suppose so. But *why*?"

"I don't know, do I? But maybe we now got an answer to the question Vance asked, about whether she gave you anything for safekeeping, although I bet he didn't know exactly what it was. So let's go back to square one, Lou."

"What's that?"

"Forget about baseball and Italian food. Think about antiques. Ivory. Japanese art. Collecting stuff. During those cozy little conversations you had, did she ever mention any of those?"

Chapter 8

Zukie actually expected a negative answer to her question, so she was surprised and delighted when Lou nodded slowly.

"You know, I'd totally forgotten about that, but now you mention it …"

"What?" Zukie was almost quivering with excitement.

"We were talking about where to go one day and she said she'd like to go out to Volunteer Park."

Zukie did a quick mental inventory of the park, one of Seattle's oldest. Among its attractions were a venerable conservatory with some rare plants, acres of gardens and tree-filled parkland, a cemetery where several city pioneers were buried, a reservoir and …

"The art museum," she said triumphantly. "I think it's all Asian art there these days, Japanese and Chinese and so on. The other stuff is downtown. Is that where you went?"

"Yeah."

Zukie deduced from that Lou had not been entranced by the museum's impressive collection. He would have vastly preferred a baseball game, followed by pizza and beer.

"And was she real interested in the *netsuke*? Or anything else in particular?"

Lou wrinkled his forehead, thinking. "Not that I remember. In fact, I don't remember seeing any of these doo-dahs there at all, but I got to admit I wasn't paying a lot of attention. Seen one

Chinese scroll, you've seen them all."

"You mean you could hardly wait to get out of there and into doing something more exciting with her." Zukie sighed in frustration. "Did she talk to anyone when you were at the museum? Spend a lot of time looking at one exhibit? Do anything out of the ordinary?"

"Not that I remember."

"What *do* you remember? Honestly, Lou, you're the world's worst witness."

"Listen, I didn't know there'd be any reason for me having to remember anything. Let's see. She bought a couple of postcards in the museum shop when we were done looking around. That's all."

"Well, that's something. But you do realize we got to tell Vance or Jim or that Corinne Holt about this, don't you? 'Cause it has to have something to do with Shirley and if she's been murdered, it might be because she stole some of those *netsuke* or welshed on paying for one or…"

"Stop." Lou held up a hand. "Call Vance and tell him. Give him the damn toggle."

"*Netsuke*."

"Whatever. Then that's the end of it, *capisc'?*"

"Jeez, Lou, you might have gotten yourself hooked up with an international art thief. That's pretty good, just from jump-starting a car at the bowling alley."

Lou scowled at her. "Just call Vance."

"OK."

Zukie reached for the phone. It said something for her relationship with Vance that his personal cell phone number was on her speed dial list, although she tried her best to keep a prudent distance between them. She would have called Jim Lanigan first, but after all, it was Vance who had been parked in front of her house and who had broken the news about Shirley. And Lanigan was on Vance's team, so he would learn about it sooner or later, and would be better informed when she got around to tackling him.

Vance obviously had Zukie on a list of some sort, too, because he answered the call by saying, "Yes, Mrs Merlino?"

"It could have been Lou calling you from this number," Zukie pointed out.

"But it's not. It's you."

"Yes, although you'll probably want to talk to him, too. He found something in his jacket pocket, something that we think Shirley Minghella stashed there."

Vance had been thinking his day couldn't get much worse, but now he reconsidered. He was going to have to deal with Mrs Merlino again.

"What is it?"

"A *netsuke*."

"A what?"

Zukie cast her eyes to the ceiling, brought them back down and embarked on a brief explanation.

"So this one looks like it's ivory and pretty old, and I know some of them are real valuable. But don't ask me why she stuck it in Lou's jacket. I mean, I can think of a bunch of reasons, but they might not be right."

It was unusual for Zukie to admit she could be wrong, and Vance seized the opportunity.

"What would be the reasons?"

"First, to ditch it because she shouldn't have had it, or didn't want it found on her. Second, to plant it on Lou, so he'd get blamed for stealing it, something like that. Third, she planned to get it back and was just hiding it for a while in case someone else was looking for it. Lou says he never uses that pocket and it's not very big, so he wouldn't have noticed. Fourth, she was using Lou as a kind of courier, and later on someone would pick his pocket or mug him, and take it. Fifth …"

"Stop," Vance pleaded. "Right. Thank you for sharing this information, Mrs Merlino. I will send Detective Holt over in a while to pick up the *netsuke*."

"OK. Anything new on Shirley?"

"Even if there was, I wouldn't be telling you," Vance said.

"Thank you again. Good-bye, Mrs Merlino."

Zukie replaced the phone and glared at it.

"What did he say?" Lou asked.

"Detective Holt's coming over to pick it up."

"Good."

"That's all you got to say?"

"What else could there be? I didn't know she stuck it in my pocket and I'll be glad to get rid of it."

"Don't you want to know why she put it there?"

"Not particularly. And she's not going to tell me, is she?"

Zukie had to concede defeat on that one. "There must be something special about it, if someone murdered her over it."

"You don't know that's why she was killed. She might have got caught in a gang shootout crossfire or something stupid like that."

That made two statements in a row that she couldn't deny the truth of, so Zukie temporarily withdrew. When Lou could out-think her, it was worrying, and time to re-draw her battle plans. However, she felt obliged to fire one last shot across his bow.

"If her death was accidental like that, Vance wouldn't be involved, would he? So I bet it was deliberate murder."

"But maybe it was nothing to do with this ivory doo-dah."

Zukie sniffed. He could be right, but she doubted it. To her way of thinking, a mature but attractive blonde who sneaked a valuable antique into the pocket of a short-term partner was someone who might very well get herself murdered. By whom was another question altogether, and not one Zukie was prepared to answer.

Rather than debate the point, she went into the kitchen and got a clean sandwich bag from the drawer. She brought it back to the living room and popped the *netsuke* inside, sealing the top shut.

"It's too bad I touched it," she said, "but the cops have got my DNA on record, I think, so they can eliminate me."

Lou refrained from saying they probably had her DNA, fingerprints, mug shots, dental records and shoe size on file, considering the amount of trouble she had caused the Seattle Police Department. Of course, she had also contributed a few helpful suggestions and even cornered a murderer or two, but on the whole, he could see why Vance steered clear of her whenever possible.

"When's this Holt coming over?" he asked.

"He said 'in a while'. So later this evening, I guess."

"Good. Now can I watch TV?"

"Go for it."

Lou switched the television on while Zukie withdrew to the kitchen, the sandwich bag clutched in one hand. She sat at the table and studied the little ivory fish through the clear plastic. It really was an attractive object, and she could understand why a collector might want it.

That didn't, however, get her any nearer to an explanation of why Shirley had secreted it in Lou's pocket. The list of reasons she had rattled off to Vance were all possibilities, but there might be something else she hadn't thought of.

While she was waiting for Holt to show up, Zukie decided she might as well deal with another aspect of the investigation. Her investigation, that is, not the police department's, even though she appreciated they might overlap.

She put the *netsuke* aside and picked up the phone.

"Hey, Ange," she said. "Any luck yet?"

"Good grief, give me a chance. You only asked me about it this afternoon, and I do have other things to do beside help you poke your nose into other people's business."

It wasn't often Angela dared speak that sharply to Zukie, but the fact that she was three miles away and on the end of a phone line probably encouraged her. For her part, Zukie faced the unpalatable truth that she needed her sister's help and backed down, but only a short way.

"Sorry. I got something else you might throw into the hopper, though."

"What's that?"

Zukie gave Angela an even briefer explanation of *netsuke*

than she had given Vance, figuring complete details weren't necessary. Angela's skills tended to be social rather than intellectual.

"How strange," Angela said.

"You're telling me. So that's something else you might kind of casually inquire about, whether anyone connected in any way with Shirley or Michael Minghella – if you find them – is interested in art or antiques. Don't specifically mention Japanese art – that would be asking for trouble."

"OK. It might take me some time, you know, being as I don't have a good place to start."

"I have faith in you, Ange," Zukie said truthfully. "You'll find something."

WHEN THE doorbell rang half an hour later, Zukie took the precaution of looking through the peephole before opening it. She didn't have many visitors after dark, and when there was a murderer on the loose who might have it in for Lou, she felt it was better to check first.

Corinne Holt stood on the porch, lit by the overhead light, so Zukie opened the door and let her in. Lou got up from the armchair and came over.

"Evening, Mr Romano," Holt said. "Detective Vance tells me you found something unusual in your jacket pocket."

"Yeah," Lou said. "And before you ask, I never saw it before, didn't know what it was and once you've taken it away, I never want to see it again."

Holt hid a smile.

"Zukie knew what those things are called," he continued, "but that's only because she reads all sorts of stuff."

Holt glanced at the coffee table, which held a neat stack of magazines including *National Geographic, Psychology Today* and *Scientific American*.

"So I see. Do you think Shirley Minghella put the *netsuke* in your pocket?"

"She must have. Nobody else was anywhere near it."

"And do you know when this happened?"

"Probably the last time I saw her, when we were at the mall. I took my jacket off in the restaurant and it was hanging on the back of my chair. I haven't worn the jacket since then, because the sleeve got ripped when I fell in the parking garage."

"Could anybody else have had access to it?"

"I don't think so. My chair was kind of in the corner, so there wasn't anybody else going past it."

"OK. Let's take a look at this *netsuke*."

Zukie went out to the kitchen and brought the sandwich bag back, handing it to Holt.

"It's kind of cute, isn't it?" she said.

"And quite valuable, I think," Holt said. "There's a market for these, especially the ivory ones."

"How valuable?" Zukie asked. Lou frowned at her, afraid she might snatch the bag back if she thought it was worth her while.

"Oh, I couldn't give you a precise figure, Mrs Merlino. It depends on the demand and the rarity. Let's just say a collection of them could run well into six figures."

"But just one on its own?"

"Much less, I suppose. I'm afraid I'm not an art or antique expert."

"But I guess you guys must be in touch with people who are. I mean, not you people in homicide, but other parts of SPD."

"Yes," Holt said. "If Shirley's death is connected to the art or antique business in any way, we'll liaise with them."

"Do you think it is?"

"We don't know at this point. It's still very early in the investigation."

Zukie would have pried some more, but she could hear Lou growling quietly, like a bear gearing up for an attack. So she just smiled and said, "Well, I hope you're successful. Thanks for coming over so quick."

"No problem. We appreciate your telling us about it."

Holt put the sandwich bag inside another evidence bag and

moved toward the door. "If anything else turns up, please let me or Detective Vance know."

"Sure," Zukie said. She opened the door for Holt and when the detective had driven off, turned to Lou with a triumphant expression.

"Now what?" he said apprehensively. "You going to tell me she's not a real cop or something? Remember she was here with Vance and he should know."

"Oh, I think she's real enough. I wouldn't have let her take it otherwise. No, it's Shirley I'm wondering about."

"Huh?"

"Well, Detective Holt called her Shirley. Vance called her Ms Minghella. Since when do cops call murder victims by their first names?"

LOU THOUGHT that one over and then said, "So what are you saying? That she was a buddy of Shirley's?"

"Nope. Think about it."

Lou's eyes widened as he realized what she was hinting. "You think Shirley was a cop?"

"Maybe. An undercover one." Zukie snickered and Lou glared at her.

"You're a riot, Zuke. She sure never said anything to make me think she was. And she said she was retired."

"People can say anything, Lou. You admit you never asked her much about herself and she didn't volunteer much. OK, she was an age where she might have been retired, 'cause I don't know if the police have a point where they kick you out and she was at least in her mid-fifties, I'd say, but on the other hand, she might still have been working for them. Or with them, if she was an art expert, something like that."

Lou cautiously picked his way through her statement and said, "She had a lot of spare time for someone who was still working, so I doubt it."

"So she might have been a kind of consultant for the police.

You know, those people who just pop in and out, give their opinion and then send you a humongous bill for five minutes' work."

Zukie spoke with a certain amount of resentment, considering she had been on minimum wage plus tips at the Plane View café, and in her opinion, she had been an unpaid consultant to the cook there. Admittedly he had never asked for her opinion, but he should have. And Carol had occasionally mentioned the role of consultants at her workplace, so Zukie had grasped the general idea.

"That would explain why she dressed nice and had her hair highlighted and a manicure and so on," she added. "She had money to burn."

"You don't know any of this," Lou pointed out. "You're just guessing."

"I know. But it makes sense, doesn't it?"

"Sort of."

"And it explains why Vance was being so closed-mouth about telling us any details about how she died. Cops close ranks when it's one of their own who gets killed."

"He didn't tell us any details because it was none of our business," Lou said. "We've given them the toggle thing now, so as far as I'm concerned, that's the end of it."

Zukie agreed in principle, but it seemed a rather inconclusive end to an intriguing series of events. Babysitting Joe was all very well, but it only provided a challenge if he decided to howl in the middle of the supermarket where people might criticize her child-minding skills. If she took him out of the equation, she was left with housework and gardening, neither of which stirred her interest much. Even cooking, which she enjoyed and used as therapy when needed, wasn't nearly as compelling as a homicide investigation.

"If you say so," she said. "But if I come across anything that might be connected to her death, I'd feel obliged to tell Vance."

"If you 'come across' anything?" Lou was understandably skeptical. "If you stir up any kind of a hornet's nest, you mean."

Zukie decided not to dignify that with a response. Instead, she asked politely, "Mind if I use your laptop for a little while?"

"Go ahead," Lou said, having learned the hard way it was better not to ask why she wanted it. Zukie had finally admitted she knew how to find her way around the internet, after several years of pretending ignorance, and had become quite adept at locating information. He never checked her browsing history, afraid of what he might find.

"Thanks."

Lou settled himself in front of the television while Zukie went into his bedroom to commune with the laptop. Her goal had originally been to find out more about *netsuke*, just in case she was involved any further in Vance's investigation. But instead, she found herself typing 'art thefts' into the search engine and then reading several accounts of heists around the world, some so brazen even she was impressed.

She jotted down a few notes of particularly interesting cases before closing the laptop and going back out to announce to Lou that she was going to take a bath. It was necessary to notify him in advance because once she was soaking in a nest of bubbles and hot water, the house's only bathroom would be inaccessible for at least half an hour, and she didn't want Lou complaining that he needed to use it.

Zukie eased herself into the bath and relaxed, letting her mind wander. She couldn't pretend to feel too distressed about Shirley's death, and she was thankful Lou seemed to be coping. After all, it wasn't as if they'd been a couple for very long, and in Zukie's eyes, someone who was so secretive didn't deserve a man as straightforward as Lou.

On the other hand, the woman didn't appear to have done anything to deserve being murdered, and that upset Zukie more than she wanted to admit. And Lou had obviously liked her – at least until the parking garage episode – so she felt obliged to do something to help bring Shirley's killer to justice.

"If I only knew where to start," she said aloud, and yanked the plug out.

Chapter 9

The following morning found Zukie up with the lark – had there been any larks in the south end of Seattle – and ready for action.

Since it was Thursday, the greater part of her day was already pre-ordained, and Carol would be bringing Joe over shortly after breakfast. So she made the most of the few moments uncluttered by other people, gazing out the kitchen window at the sunrise while she ate her toast and drank her first cup of coffee.

It was one of her favorite activities, even though it didn't last long, reminding her that however frustrating or depressing things might seem at the moment, the sun would rise every day and life would go on.

She was pleased to see today's sunrise was a five-star production, painting the eastern sky over the Cascade Mountains with streaks of brilliant red and purple, fading to pink at the edges. Zukie decided to take that as a good omen, and when she heard Lou beginning to move around in his bedroom, she gave the sky a last appreciative glance and went to the stove.

Eight minutes later – Zukie always timed him and he was rarely off – Lou lumbered into the kitchen and muttered a greeting. He never understood how his cousin could hit the ground running every morning, but then he was usually not there early enough to see the sun come up.

He was glad that she did, however, since it meant he could sit down to a cooked breakfast on all but the hottest days. Today it was two fried eggs, sausage links and toast, accompanied by a slice of cantaloupe and a cup of coffee, and Lou threw her a silent look of gratitude before digging in.

By the time his plate was empty and she had re-filled their coffee cups, he was capable of coherent speech, and asked, "What are you doing today? Have you got Joe?"

"I will when Carol drops him off. I might take him with me to the supermarket. He likes riding in the cart and looking around."

"And you like showing him off."

"Anything wrong with that?"

"I guess not. I'm going over to Lynn's and then I'll probably meet up with Dave and Neal for lunch."

"At the Plane View?"

A slightly frosty silence descended over the table, broken by Lou saying, "I think I'll be safe enough, Zukie, with three of us together. And I promise I won't offer to help anybody, even if they're crawling across the parking lot with a broken leg and half a dozen bullet holes in them."

"That should be all right, then," Zukie said, ignoring the sarcasm. "I'll see you when you get back."

The doorbell rang and she went to answer it, seeing Carol through the peephole, Joe balanced on her hip.

"Hi, sweetie," Zukie said. Joe squealed happily.

"You sure you're all right having him today?" Carol asked, stepping inside.

"Why wouldn't I be?"

Carol frowned at her mother. "I thought you might need to take Lou somewhere."

"He can take himself. What are you talking about?"

"I guess you haven't looked at the driveway this morning."

Zukie detoured around Carol and went out onto the front porch. Lou's Buick sat in its normal place in the driveway, but in somewhat different condition than when he had parked it there. The driver's side door hung open, and even from the porch, Zukie could see that both the front and back seats had been

86

ripped open, with the filling strewn around and springs visible. Her hand shot up to cover her mouth.

"Holy saints," she whispered. She went back into the living room, where Lou was tickling Joe's chin.

"Better call your insurance company," she told him.

"Why?"

"Go take a look at your car."

Lou obeyed and came back a minute later, his face contorted in anger.

"Who the hell did that?"

Joe began to cry.

"Now look what you've done," Zukie said. "Jeez, Lou, it's not like it's much of a mystery. Random thugs don't rip up car seats; they key the paintwork or steal the hubcaps. So offhand, I'd guess it's the same guy, or guys, who killed Shirley." She looked at Carol, who was bouncing Joe to distract him from Lou's wrath. "Did you know that she was dead?"

"Yes, Jim told me. He probably shouldn't have, but since Lou was involved, he did."

"Just as well. Now as for the car, I bet someone was looking for something in it, and I'll give you one guess what it was."

Carol looked blank, but Lou groaned. "Oh, God, not that again. But I don't have it, and when I *did* have it, I didn't know I had it."

"That sounds like one of Mom's explanations," Carol said. "What don't you have, Lou?"

"A little ivory Japanese gizmo worth big bucks. I gave it to Detective Holt to give to Vance."

"Ah, I see. But someone didn't know that, and thought you still had it, maybe hidden in the car."

"Right," Zukie said, pleased that her daughter had inherited some deductive skills. "And we think Shirley must have put it in Lou's jacket pocket, 'cause that's where it was."

"But now the police have it."

"Right again."

"So report this to them, and then call your insurance

company."

"You make it sound so easy," Zukie said, taking Joe from Carol. "It's way more complicated than that."

"That's why there's a police department, Mom, so stay out of it." She gave Joe a kiss. "Bye, sweetheart. Be a good boy for Grandma and I'll see you this afternoon."

She was gone before Zukie could formulate a reply. Behind her, Lou was predicting gloomily that his insurance premium would go up when none of it was his fault, and not only that, but he'd be without a car for who knew how long.

"Carol's right, I suppose," Zukie said, shifting Joe to her hip and picking up his bag of bottles and diapers. "Call Vance first. His number's on speed dial."

"It would be," Lou muttered, but he picked up the phone.

Zukie took Joe into the kitchen to put his bottles in the fridge. She could hear Lou telling someone – possibly Vance himself – what had happened to the car, and the words, "Damn right I'm upset about it," which didn't bode well. Generally speaking, Lou was far more patient and level-headed than Zukie, but even he could get riled about a car with gutted seats.

"It's OK; Uncle Lou will calm down in a little while, so don't you worry," she told Joe, who looked at her with solemn brown eyes. "And besides, Grandma will find out who made such a mess of his car."

Joe gurgled in agreement and Zukie carried him back into the living room.

"What did Vance say?"

"Not to touch the car until they've had someone come out and take pictures and dust it for prints and check for DNA. As if I could drive it anyway like that, with no seat left to sit on. He seems to have an idea who did this, Zuke, and I'm betting it wasn't Shirley."

"Of course it wasn't. So I guess you're stuck here for the time being."

"Unless I want to walk to Lynn's, which I don't."

"We'll work something out, Lou."

"Jeez, thanks. I'll wash the dishes while I'm waiting for the cops."

He stalked off to the kitchen and Zukie listened, hoping he wouldn't hurl the breakfast dishes to the floor in anger. She put Joe down on his back on the living room carpet, where he promptly rolled over onto his stomach and tried to hoist himself up on his hands and knees, only to nose dive again.

Zukie grinned at him.

"You'll be crawling before long, Joe," she said. "It's not too hard once you get the hang of it. You just move one leg and one arm at a time, not everything at once."

It occurred to her that was a reasonable description of her own activity at the moment. Work out one part of the mystery at a time, and then with luck, it would all begin to come together and she could move forward. Of course, the police might get there first, but for once, Zukie didn't care. Keeping Lou out of danger was the most important thing.

When the doorbell rang a few minutes later, she scooped Joe up and looked out the window. A vehicle she recognized as Vance's unmarked car stood at the curb, so she opened the door, to find him and Detective Holt on the porch. Behind her, Lou was muttering dire threats and she barely restrained herself from kicking him. If he hadn't been such a sucker for a sob story in the first place, none of this would have happened.

"Hi there," she said to the police officers. "Do you want to come in or are you just here to look at the car?"

"Mostly the car," Vance said. "We may have a few questions for Mr Romano later."

Joe hid his face against Zukie's shoulder, just peering up enough to see the strange people.

"Oh, he's adorable," Holt said. "He's Jim Lanigan's little boy, isn't he?"

Since she wanted to stay on Holt's good side, Zukie bit her tongue to keep from replying that Carol had also had something to do with producing Joe. She managed a smile.

"Yes, this is Joe."

"He's so sweet. Is Grandma baby-sitting you today, Joe?"

Lou and Vance were in total agreement for once, exchanging exasperated male glances.

"If you can tear yourself away, Holt, let's look at this damaged car," Vance said.

Holt grinned at Zukie and followed Vance and Lou over to the car. Left in the house, Zukie debated what her next move should be. She might have to transport Lou somewhere, that much was clear, but there should be something else she could tackle as well.

Nothing came to mind immediately, so she paced the floor with Joe, darting an occasional glance out of the window. A forensic van had arrived now, and a couple of technicians were circling the Buick cautiously, first taking photographs and then examining it more closely for any clues it might hold.

As always, Zukie was fascinated by watching them work and only tore herself away because the telephone began to ring.

"Yeah?"

"That's no way to answer the phone," Angela said.

"Well, I'm kind of busy at the moment, Ange, in between having Joe here and watching the police forensic guys deal with Lou's car."

As she had expected, that stopped Angela in her tracks.

"The police are looking at Lou's car? What happened to it?"

"Somebody vandalized it. Ripped the seats up."

"Why?"

"Think about it."

Angela thought about it. "They were looking for that Japanese thingy."

"*Netsuke*," Zukie said. "For Pete's sake, Ange, it's not that hard to remember. Why are you calling, anyway? Have you found out something?"

"I'm not sure."

"What is it?"

"I remembered where I heard the name Minghella."

"That's something. Where?"

"There's a company called Minghella something or another not too far from Safeco Field. A factory of some kind, I think. We drove past it once when we were going to a Mariners game."

Zukie sat down and settled Joe onto her lap. "OK, that's a start."

"There might not be any connection," Angela warned.

"I know that, but it's not that common a name. Do you know anything about it, or the people who run it?"

"No, but Ray might know. I'll ask him tonight. I would have asked him earlier but I only just thought of it."

Zukie chafed at the idea of having to wait until Angela's husband came home from work to provide any other clues, but at least this was a glimmer of hope.

"What kind of stuff does this Minghella place make?" she asked.

"How would I know? We just drove past and it's not like I knew you were going to want to know about them. "

"I suppose not," Zukie conceded. "It'd be good if you could remember, though. Never mind; I'll talk to you later, 'cause the cops are coming back to the house now. Thanks."

She hung up as the front door opened and Lou came in, followed by Vance and Holt.

"I'll have to call the insurance people and see if I can get a loaner," Lou said. "This is so stupid."

Zukie agreed, but felt this was not the time to discuss it. "Did you find anything?" she asked Vance.

"We'll have to get the forensics report first," he said. "Mr Romano says you didn't hear any unusual activity last night."

"Nope. Guess they were pretty quiet about it."

"It would seem so."

"And since they didn't find anything in the car, they might try the house next."

Vance twitched slightly. He had hoped Zukie wouldn't think of that, but he should have known better.

"It's possible. Do you have an alarm system?"

"Heck, no. I have nosy neighbors. Works just as well and it's a lot cheaper."

Holt smothered a grin and Vance said, "But probably not as effective. I don't think your neighbors are watching the house twenty-four seven, and besides, where were they last night while Mr Romano's car was being vandalized?"

That was a low blow, and Zukie took it on the chin.

"OK, you got a point. What happens next?"

"When forensics are done with the car, Mr Romano needs to contact his insurance company and report the damage. No details, no mention of Japanese antiques; just that a person or persons unknown decided it would be amusing to break into the car and rip up the seats. We'll give you a report you can submit to them."

"Thanks," Lou muttered.

"Then we'll get you set up right away with a temporary security system, something basic that will detect movement and send us an alarm call if it goes off. I've already asked the tech team to send someone out, so they'll be here shortly. It won't take too long to set it up."

"My neighbors will think I've finally lost it," Zukie said. "They'll think I'm spying on them."

"You *do* spy on them," Lou said.

"It won't be obvious, and our technicians are discreet," Vance said. "Now, a rather personal question, Mr Romano."

"What's that?"

"Could Shirley Minghella have left anything else with you before your final scene with her? We'll assume she didn't leave anything in your car, but how about anywhere else? Clothing, personal belongings?"

Zukie didn't dare look at Lou, having suddenly visualized Shirley trying to find a hiding place for a small ivory figurine during their more intimate moments.

"I don't think she did, but of course, I wasn't looking out for that."

"No, of course not. Obviously, if you come across anything else, contact us right away."

"Yeah. Sure."

Zukie decided to take a short cut, one that would save hours of possibly fruitless research or snooping on her part.

"So do you guys think she was stealing the *netsuke*? I mean, it's not the kind of thing most people would be carrying around in their pocket or purse."

Vance and Holt exchanged glances.

"No, we don't think she stole it," Vance said finally. "Let's leave it like that, all right?"

"Now wait just a minute," Zukie said, moving to stand between him and the front door. For good measure, she held Joe up, just to remind them there was a small, defenseless person involved.

"Lou's car's been ripped up, you are worried enough about someone breaking in here to install a security system for us, and you won't tell us what's going on? I may not be the sharpest tack around, but I get the feeling there's something very funny about Shirley Minghella and I don't exactly think you're giving us the whole picture, are you?"

A complete silence followed this declaration. Lou looked at his cousin with a combination of admiration and apprehension. Although Vance's face stayed more or less impassive, Holt appeared more flustered, possibly because she had only known Zukie a short time. Even Joe seemed impressed, staring up at his grandmother with wide brown eyes.

Vance locked gazes with Zukie. He might have faced numerous murderers, but Zukie had stood up to three aggressive older brothers during her formative years, and it took a lot to intimidate her. Vance wasn't up to the challenge. As she had hoped, he came to the conclusion that giving her a limited amount of information would keep her from ferreting around and causing him more headaches.

"Sit down," he ordered her.

Zukie bristled a little at that, considering she was in her own house. She tried to calculate whether she could still get between him and the door if she retreated to the sofa, especially when handicapped by holding Joe.

"Only if you tell us what's going on."

"Please sit down, Mrs Merlino."

That was better. Zukie edged over to the sofa and perched on it, Joe on her lap. Lou sat in the armchair opposite and glared at her.

"Go on, then," she said to Vance.

"I suppose this is a ridiculous thing to ask, but I'd appreciate it if you didn't share what I'm about to tell you with anyone else. That includes your sister."

Zukie raised her eyebrows and refrained from saying that if it was anything worthy of gossip, Angela probably already knew about it.

"Sure. I understand."

"All right. I hope you also understand that I can't give you all the details, just enough to …"

"Shut me up?"

"Good luck with that," Lou grumbled.

"Enough to paint a picture, let's say. Then I would hope you would exercise common sense."

Lou started to speak, but stopped himself.

"OK," Zukie said. "Shoot."

Vance cleared his throat and looked at Lou. "The woman you knew as Shirley Minghella was not exactly the person she represented herself to you as."

"We worked that one out," Zukie said. "It's kind of obvious. Was she a cop?"

Both Vance and Holt stared at her. Vance recovered first.

"She was working with SPD," he said. "It's not the same thing."

"Working with you doing what?"

"Sharing some specialized expertise."

"Something to do with Japanese antiques, I guess."

"Yes." Vance hesitated, then plunged ahead. "There's quite a market for *netsuke*, and some, as I think you know, are worth thousands of dollars to collectors. And because they're small and portable, that makes them very attractive to art thieves."

"I get it," Zukie said. "It's not like trotting off with the Mona Lisa, is it? If you got your hands on a bunch of valuable *netsuke*, you could walk away with a million bucks worth in your pockets, and if you were lucky, no one would even notice, for a while, at least. Is that what happened?"

Chapter 10

"Not exactly," Vance said, "although you're not too far off."

Zukie preened herself. Lou looked pole-axed.

"Are you trying to say I got myself mixed up with some million-dollar art theft? And Shirley was part of it?"

"You're not listening," Zukie told him. "She was one of the good guys. That's probably why she was murdered."

This news didn't noticeably impress Lou.

"OK, so I got mixed up with someone who was trying to catch someone who stole a bunch of these Japanese things and got herself murdered for her trouble. That's not much better, especially since these guys seem to think she … hold on a minute. If she wasn't a thief, what was she doing with the *netsuke* she planted on me?"

Zukie bestowed a radiant smile on her cousin. It was partly because he had finally used the correct term for the *netsuke* and partly because he had asked precisely the right question.

"Good question, Lou," she said encouragingly.

"And not one I'm prepared to answer at the moment," Vance said. "I'm not being difficult; I don't know why she had it and I don't know why she, as you say, planted it on you. Nor do I know who tried to hit you in the parking garage, or even if that is connected. But as Mrs Merlino so correctly says, Shirley was one of the good guys, and we intend to find her killer and bring them to justice."

Zukie was tempted to applaud, since it was one of the very few times Vance had given her any credit for anything, at least in her hearing. She contented herself with smiling modestly.

"What's her real name?" she asked. "Is it Minghella?"

"I believe it's her ex-husband's name," Holt said. "So I suppose you could say so."

"Some women go back to using their maiden names after they're divorced."

"So I understand," Holt said, having caught a warning glance from Vance. Zukie caught it, too, and decided not to press her luck.

"What happens now?" she asked. "You're going to give me a security alarm and then what? Hope someone tries to break in here?"

"I wouldn't go quite that far," Vance said. "But we will be prepared, and if someone does try, we'll be here within minutes."

"Gosh."

"In the meantime, I suggest you get Mr Romano's transportation problems sorted out. We'll e-mail you a copy of the official report of the vandalism that you can give to your insurer."

"I guess that'll have to do," Lou said. "They probably wouldn't believe me if I told them the truth."

WHEN Vance and Holt had gone, Lou phoned his insurance company while Zukie sat on the sofa and gave Joe his mid-morning bottle. The excitement hadn't affected him at all, she was pleased to see, and he was glugging down the last drops when Lou finished his call and then went to his bedroom to check the e-mail.

She heard the printer whirring and then he came out holding some papers.

"Got it," he said. "They're going to come and tow the car and leave me a loaner. So that's not too bad."

"And I suppose the police guys will be here before too long to put up the alarm system. Wonder if they'll let me keep it."

"I doubt it, knowing what Vance thinks of you."

"You got to admit it could be useful."

"Zukie, you're not allowed to turn the camera around to spy on the neighbors."

"I wasn't going to do that," Zukie said, wondering if it was indeed possible. She put Joe over her shoulder and patted his back until he burped noisily. "Keep an eye on the door, will you?"

"There's not much else I *can* do," Lou said under his breath. He stationed himself by the door while Zukie took Joe into the bedroom to change his wet diaper, the inevitable aftermath of a full bottle of milk.

By the time she returned, an unmarked van had parked in front of the house and two technicians were on the front porch, holding a quiet but intense conversation with Lou. Zukie promptly butted in, since it was her house, and besides, she was curious.

"What are you doing?" she asked. "What are those things?"

"These are just basic motion activated cameras," one of the technicians told her. "We'll put one at the front and one at the back. They'll be linked to the precinct, so we can see if anything triggers them."

"You mean you'll be spying on us?"

"Not exactly. Detective Vance assumes you won't be burglarizing your own house."

"What if I go out in the evening?" Lou asked.

"We'll be able to see it's you."

"Oh."

"You OK with that?" the technician asked.

"Guess we'll have to be," Zukie said. "Go for it."

Vance had been right when he had said it wouldn't take long to install the cameras. In fact, the work was done so quickly that Zukie was tempted to ask if they were real cameras designed to catch prospective burglars or just dummy ones to pacify her and

Lou. And Vance had also been right when he promised they would be discreet, tucked away in a corner of the front porch and over the back door.

In a way, she was disappointed, having half hoped for something a bit flashier and more high tech. One that flooded the area with bright lights and sirens when activated would have been more like it. Or maybe a force field that would immobilize any intruder.

She listened as the technicians ran a final check, speaking to someone in what sounded like a foreign language, being loaded with abbreviations and acronyms. They packed up their equipment and drove off, leaving Zukie and Lou looking at each other and wondering what to do next. Zukie began to fidget.

"You OK waiting here for the insurance company to turn up?" she said. "I hate sitting around here doing nothing."

"Yeah, go on," Lou said. "I don't really have a choice, do I? I'll call you if anything happens."

"OK. Thanks. Come on, Joe, we're going for a ride in the car."

Getting herself to the supermarket, or indeed anywhere, was a considerably more complex affair when Joe was with her, so despite Lou's cooperation, it took Zukie a while to get under way. Once Joe was securely fastened into his car seat, however, and the bag of baby equipment stowed away, she pulled out of the driveway and headed for the supermarket, driving much more sedately than her normal pace.

Having Joe with her also made the usually uneventful shopping trip more of an adventure, in Zukie's opinion. There would be opportunities to show him off if she encountered anyone she knew, or even to total strangers, along with the challenge of keeping him from reaching out and grabbing items off the shelves.

She carried him inside and tucked him into the shopping cart's baby carrier basket, wishing something similar had been available when Carol was small, instead of having to juggle a stroller with one hand and the cart with the other. Modern mothers have it so easy in some ways, she thought, even if it does take two incomes to make ends meet. Slinging her purse strap over the cart handle, she started down the first aisle.

Since she had already done her major shopping for the week, Zukie contented herself with some leisurely browsing. She wandered through the produce section, pretending not to notice the manager scuttling for the storeroom when he spotted her. They were always at loggerheads, thanks to the store's policy of spraying the vegetable displays occasionally to keep them looking fresh.

Zukie strongly disapproved of this practice, having been caught in the face several times while reaching for a head of lettuce or bunch of carrots, and had once turned the sprinklers on the manager in retaliation. It had been enough to make him stay a prudent distance away whenever she was in his part of the store, or if forced to speak to her, to do it out of range of the sprayers.

She picked out an avocado, a bunch of grapes, two lemons and a green pepper to justify her presence and then moved on to the clothing section, where she chose a red and white striped T-shirt for Joe.

"What do you think?" she asked him, holding it up. "It's my high school colors."

Joe squealed and tried to grab the shirt.

"OK, Grandma will buy it for you. Now let's go get some milk."

She pushed the cart to the back of the store, where she was forced to wait by the chilled dairy cabinets while two elderly women held a discussion on the merits of the various types of milk available.

"It all has vitamin D in it," one of them said.

"I heard they add something else, too," the other woman said darkly. "You don't know what you're putting on your cereal these days. It could be anything."

"And what's the point of having both one per cent and two percent fat? It's not like you can taste the difference."

"Oh, I know. As long as it's not skim milk. I never buy that. You might as well use water. It looks like milk, I know, but it's not the real thing."

Zukie was never patient at the best of times, and she resented having to listen to two strangers discussing the merits of dairy products, even if she agreed with them. She was tempted to suggest they just grab a carton and get out of her way when a thought struck her, triggered by the last comment.

"Now I wonder," she said thoughtfully.

Both women turned to look at her.

"Nothing to do with milk," Zukie said hastily. "Just hand me a carton of two percent, will you?"

VANCE HAD returned to the precinct from Zukie's house in a bad mood. He had hoped to remove Lou completely from the case, but a badly vandalized car was too much to ignore. Especially, he reasoned, since the vandals had either been looking for something hidden in it, or more likely, trying to throw a scare into Lou.

It wasn't that Vance didn't believe Lou's story; he was far more concerned that someone else hadn't. He had been somewhat shaken by Zukie's quick analysis of the situation, too, and yet he told himself he should have expected it. The woman was always a nuisance, but an intelligent nuisance.

On that thought, he summoned Zukie's son-in-law, hoping he might possess some extra insight into the workings of her mind.

Jim Lanigan was tall and lanky, with a shock of bushy brown hair. Zukie had been privately thankful Joe had inherited his mother's smooth dark hair, although she liked Lanigan immensely and would never have expressed this sentiment to his face.

He presented himself to Vance, who waved at a chair. Lanigan sat. He had a feeling he knew what was coming, since Carol had told him about the vandalized car, but he waited patiently while Vance outlined the latest developments.

"So this is getting complicated," Vance said. "Why in God's name Shirley had to hook up with Lou Romano, of all people, we will never know, but she did. In fact, it looked like she deliberately targeted him. Now I know Romano's a nice guy," he said, as Lanigan seemed about to speak, "but that's just too much of a coincidence."

"It could be," Lanigan said, "that she was on the lookout for someone like Lou – someone normal, ordinary, unlikely to arouse anyone's suspicions. That's assuming she was using him for something other than companionship."

"She wouldn't have picked him to use for anything if she knew who he shared a house with," Vance said.

"No, probably not."

"And why rip up the car seats anyway? If he – or she – had hidden something in his car, they would have put it in a more accessible place than buried in the upholstery."

"I agree. So unless the vandals are complete idiots, it was intended more as a warning, or a threat, than a serious effort to find anything. I'm pretty sure Zukie has worked that out, too."

"So our job is to try to stay one step ahead of her. Hopefully the security system we put in will discourage anyone from trying the same trick on the house. How did your esteemed mother-in-law happen to know anything about Japanese antiques in the first place?"

Lanigan grinned. "How does she happen to know about anything? She reads a lot and suffers from terminal curiosity. And now that she's discovered the joys of the internet, there's no stopping her. Say what you like, but she's never boring."

"I won't argue with that."

"And smart, too."

"Don't I know it," Vance said, with a heartfelt sigh. "It didn't take her long to figure out Shirley was working with SPD, so that also means she knows we won't let up on this."

"Did you give her any details, sir?"

"No, and I hope Holt didn't, either. Bad enough we hire an Asian art expert who's trying to play both sides against the middle, but who manages to get herself shot before she could get to the final take down ... I don't know quite how we're going to handle this."

Lanigan nodded. "Or how we're going to keep Zukie out of it. She and Lou argue a lot, but he's family, and I'm afraid all the clichés about Italian families are more or less true in her case."

Vance felt his headache getting worse.

"Will she listen to you? Heaven knows she won't listen to me."

"She might. I can try."

"Do it. That's an order. I won't have a second woman getting killed because she's too damn nosy."

BY THE time Zukie returned from the supermarket, the insurance company representative had arrived with the loaner car and the Buick was being hooked up to a tow truck. This meant Zukie had to park on the street in front of the house, which she didn't mind too much, as at least it meant progress was being made.

Lou was standing on the front walk, silently watching the operation. Zukie unstrapped Joe from his car seat and went to join him.

"That didn't take long."

"Probably means they have me on a list of troublemakers."

"Lou, that's not true. I'm the one who had the last claim, when that little twerp broke my car window."

"Good thing we have different insurers, or they'd have this address blacklisted."

Zukie recognized a bad attitude when she encountered one.

"OK, let me know if I can do anything," she said. "If you can hang onto Joe for a second, I'll get the bags out of the car."

She handed Joe to Lou before he could object, reasoning that holding a small cuddly person would improve his mood. It seemed to work, since Lou was smiling again when she returned from unpacking the groceries and Joe's T-shirt.

"Thanks," she said, taking Joe back. "You know, Lou, I could really get to like this grandmother stuff."

"And this from the woman who always sneered at people cooing over their grandkids."

"Well, I don't any more. Come on, Joe, let's go in the house and find you something to play with."

Lou followed her inside just long enough to collect his jacket, while Zukie gave Joe his favorite toy, a small stuffed rabbit.

"There's Bunny," she told him. Joe grabbed it and began to suck the rabbit's ears. "Where are you off to, Lou?"

"I'm going to pretend this is a normal day and go on over to meet the guys for lunch," he said. "I might stop at Lynn's on the way back."

"OK. Let me know if there are any problems."

"There won't be," Lou said firmly. "See you later."

Zukie watched him drive off in the courtesy car and then took Joe into Lou's bedroom, laying him on his back on the bed while she logged on to his laptop. It took her only a few minutes to find the information she was looking for, even though her long-neglected typing skills hadn't kept pace with her new IT knowledge. She studied the relevant website thoughtfully.

"Plastics," she said aloud. "Industrial molded plastics. This is starting to make a little more sense now. Don't you think so, Joe?"

There was no response and she turned her head. Joe, apparently tired of watching her struggle with the keyboard, had gone to sleep in the middle of Lou's bed, clutching his stuffed rabbit in one hand. Zukie smiled at him and went back to the screen.

AT THE precinct, Vance was also looking at a computer screen, and his expression was not nearly as complacent as Zukie's. He got up and went to the door of his office.

"Holt!"

Corinne Holt came down the corridor at a trot. "Yes, sir?"

"Come look at this."

Holt came around the end of the desk and looked at what Vance had been viewing.

"What … that can't be right."

"Apparently it is. They wouldn't make a mistake on something like that. Did you take a good look at it?"

Holt frowned. "I didn't put it under a microscope, but yes, I looked at it closely."

"And you had no suspicions?"

"No, sir."

Vance jabbed a pen in the direction of the screen.

"So tell me, Holt; why are we now looking at a forensic report telling us that what we – and presumably Shirley Minghella – thought was a valuable Japanese antique *netsuke* is a hunk of modern plastic worth at best about five bucks?"

Chapter 11

"But did she think that?" Holt asked. "From what the art guys say, not to mention that fact that she was shot, we know she wasn't exactly sticking to the script. So could she have substituted this fake for the real *netsuke*?"

"It's possible," Vance said. "She'd have had to get someone to make it, though, and get it good enough to pass muster."

"At first glance, anyway. You're right; someone did a really good job with it, but an expert would have known it wasn't authentic. And she was an expert."

"I think I feel a migraine coming on. Round everyone up, Holt, and I'll give the art guys a call. We need to pool our knowledge."

ZUKIE WAS pleased with her discovery, which seemed to at least be a pointer in the right direction. She carefully put a light blanket over Joe and went back into the kitchen to make a cup of coffee.

Even without a detailed forensic report like the one Vance was looking at, Zukie had felt there was a flaw in the conclusion they had all drawn. Someone knowledgeable about antiques would not have simply relinquished a valuable one to a man who was, after all, almost a stranger to her.

That still held true when she considered that Lou hadn't known the *netsuke* had been left in his jacket. It could easily have been discovered, fallen out or been put through a washing machine, none of which would have been helpful. It was a risk that couldn't be taken, not if the *netsuke* was worth thousands of dollars.

Therefore, it wasn't as valuable as she or Holt had thought, and learning that the Minghella business Angela had seen was a plastics manufacturer put the seal on it, in Zukie's opinion. She finished her coffee and reached for the telephone.

Fortunately, Vance had finished his briefing before his phone rang, or his team might have been treated to some new and creative profanity. As it was, he held the phone just far enough away that Zukie couldn't hear the words that escaped his lips before he could stop them.

"So I bet it isn't ivory at all," she was saying. "Or if it is, it's new and not an antique. It's just been made to look old. Somebody did a good job on it, didn't they? It looked like real old ivory, that's for sure."

"How the hell did you … no, don't tell me."

"Don't you want to know why I think it's a fake?"

Vance reconsidered his previous statement. Although he distrusted Zukie, he was forced to admit she drew the correct conclusions – or stumbled over the truth, as he preferred to think of it – an astonishing number of times. If the Mariners had her batting average, they would have aced the World Series every season.

"All right. Why did you think that?"

Zukie decided to leave Angela out of the equation. It wasn't fair, but it was simpler.

"There's a company not too far from Safeco Field called Minghella Plastics. I looked them up on the internet. I don't know for sure what kind of plastics they make or sell, but I just thought maybe someone connected with it – maybe Shirley Minghella herself – had managed to make a plastic copy of the *netsuke* that was good enough to fool someone."

"Fool who?" Zukie heard Vance's pen scratching, probably as he jotted down the company name for further investigation. She was surprised he hadn't found it already, but then he didn't have Angela on his team.

"Well, I don't know, do I? I mean, I don't even know what the heck she was doing for you guys, since you won't tell me, but it looks to me like she was caught up in the middle of some kind of art theft. Don't know if she was the thief or the person it got stolen from, or if she was fencing the stuff or trying to catch the thieves, but somehow or another ..."

"Stop," Vance pleaded. He reached in his desk drawer for his migraine pills.

Zukie obeyed, but only long enough for him to gulp down two tablets with a cup of lukewarm coffee.

"And what I really want to know is why she sucked Lou into it."

"I think we'd all like to know that, Mrs Merlino. Did he get in touch with the insurance company about his car?"

"Yep, and they gave him a loaner. Still doesn't answer my question, does it?"

"Which question was that? I'm afraid I've lost track."

"Was the *netsuke* she planted on Lou a fake? I'm guessing it was, from the way you're acting."

Vance sighed so loudly Zukie could hear it over the phone.

"Yes, it was."

"Thought so. Where's the real stuff? I guess there must be some real stuff."

"If I knew that, I wouldn't be wasting time discussing it with you," Vance snapped, before he could stop himself.

"Is that nice? Jeez, I'm only trying to help, telling you about that company."

Vance reminded himself he was an experienced police detective and Zukie was only an irritating civilian with a knack for intruding into his investigations. Or to put it slightly more courteously, a civilian with an irritating knack for intrusion.

"I appreciate the information, Mrs Merlino."

"That's better. So are you going to tell us now what happened to Shirley?"

"No. You don't need to know. To be frank, the further you stay out of this, the safer you and Mr Romano will be. I don't want a second – or third – death on my conscience."

Zukie considered this. He sounded like he meant it, and of course, she didn't want to deprive Joe of a grandmother. On cue, a howl of outrage came from the bedroom and she said hastily, "Sorry, gotta go. If there's anything else you want help with, just give me a call."

She put the phone down and went to retrieve Joe, who stopped in mid-wail and looked up at her indignantly.

"Sorry, sweetie. Grandma got a little carried away talking to that nice Mr Vance, your daddy's boss."

She picked him up and debated with herself. Had she been on her own, the next move would have been to check out the Minghella business, but she wasn't about to take Joe along on a fact-finding mission that might turn sour. There was no way of knowing how deeply, if at all, the business itself was involved in whatever Shirley had been up to. And if her ex-husband was the Minghella in question, all sorts of other factors also would come into play.

Not only that, but even Zukie's fertile brain balked at coming up with a cover story that might lead to finding out whether anyone at the business moonlighted as a manufacturer of fake antiques. So she reluctantly decided she might have to leave that line of inquiry to the police.

The other piece of information she had learned from Vance, regardless of whether he meant her to learn it, was that somewhere along the line, there had been a theft of *netsuke* and possibly other valuable items as well.

Would it have been reported in the local media? Not necessarily, if the owner had asked that it not be made public, or more importantly, if the police thought publicizing the theft would jeopardize their chances of recovering the haul.

So that, Zukie decided, was the point at which Shirley had been roped in, probably as an expert on Oriental art and antiques. Was she a real expert or only posing as one for some dishonest reason of her own? It had to be assumed she was genuine, because if the police had hired her, surely they would have checked her background and credentials thoroughly.

Shirley's background. That brought her back to Minghella Plastics. She rather regretted telling Vance about the company, but he probably would have discovered it on his own, sooner or later. She had just speeded things up a little.

On that virtuous thought, she took Joe into the kitchen and plonked him into his high chair. She mixed up a little baby cereal for him and wondered just how difficult it would be to create a plastic *netsuke* good enough that it could temporarily fool someone. Fairly difficult, she was sure. But it could be done. It *had* been done. The question was: Who needed to be fooled?

It couldn't have been Shirley herself. It probably wasn't the original owner, because who would bother to collect something that was neither authentic nor valuable? A collector would know what he or she was collecting. So the only answer was the thief or thieves. But when had they been fooled? Before the theft or afterwards, when they took a better look at what they'd stolen? And their reaction when they found out? Zukie thought she might know the answer to that one, something involving speeding cars in parking garages.

She fed Joe his cereal, managing to get at least half of it into his mouth, since Joe regarded the spoon as a toy rather than a means of conveying nourishment, and tried to grab it at every mouthful. By the time she had scraped the last spoonful out of the bowl, she had decided that it was time to turn the screw on Joe's father. If he and Carol wanted a free babysitter once a week, the least he could do was provide that babysitter with some useful information.

"There you go, Sweetie, all gone," she told Joe, who belatedly decided to cooperate and opened his mouth again. She displayed the empty bowl. "No more cereal."

Zukie lifted Joe out of the chair, and as she did, a thought hit her with an almost physical impact.

How had the thieves – if she could call them that – known where Lou lived and where his car would be? He said he hadn't told Shirley anything other than near the high school, which encompassed a fairly wide area. And his probably wasn't the only dark blue Buick in that neighborhood. It would be almost amusing if his car had, after all, been the target of some random thugs armed with utility knives, rather than a gang of international art thieves.

Zukie stifled a chuckle, because it really wasn't all that funny, and Vance would be furious if he had wasted time and money putting a pointless security system on the house. Besides, the knowledge of Lou's address didn't need to have come directly from Shirley. He had to be listed in various other places, from the voters' registration to his bowling league. A determined person, such as herself, could find it without too much effort.

Not only that, but when Zukie cast her mind back, she remembered asking Lou, in Shirley's presence, whether he'd be home for dinner. So it was obvious they lived at the same address, and her name appeared on as many lists as his. Zukie kicked herself mentally for being so gabby, but how the heck was she to know the woman would get herself murdered?

She was distracted from her musings by the click of the mail slot, and went into the living room to collect the four pieces of mail from the mat inside the front door. Two were junk mail, which went straight into the wastepaper basket, since Zukie didn't consider it worth the trouble of recycling. One was a packet of coupons from the supermarket, which could be considered a bribe.

And the fourth piece of mail was a postcard, with a color photograph of several *netsuke* on it.

ZUKIE froze, holding the postcard between thumb and forefinger. Lou's words came back to her; Shirley had purchased a couple of postcards in the art museum's shop before they left. She very carefully turned the card over. Sure enough, the information on the back identified the photograph as being of an exhibit at the museum.

The card was addressed to Lou, but Zukie had no qualms at all about reading it. Obviously the sender knew Lou's name and address, and it was almost certainly from Shirley. Since a car in her own driveway had been attacked and the police thought it possible her house was the next target, Zukie reasoned that justified her curiosity. Besides, Lou wouldn't be home for at least an hour and wouldn't mind.

Lou, she read, *keep this and remember what I said. S.*

Zukie stared at the message.

"What the heck is that supposed to mean?" she said aloud. Joe gave her a quizzical look, as if to remind her he didn't understand grown-up questions.

"Lou said she didn't say anything to him about the *netsuke*. He didn't even know what it was. So what the heck is she talking about? Something besides the *netsuke*? Or is this some kind of code? Or a joke, even?"

No one answered her questions, so Zukie took the postcard into the kitchen and put it into a clean plastic sandwich bag. She realized that it had probably been handled by numerous postal employees, but there was no reason to let it get contaminated further.

The question was what to do with it. Eventually it would have to go to the police, but if there was any way of obtaining a clue from it, Zukie was going to make the effort. She went back to Lou's bedroom, balanced Joe on her lap and propped the bagged postcard against the laptop.

This research was far more difficult than identifying the Minghella factory, and she grew increasingly frustrated. What good was the internet if she couldn't get the information she needed, more or less instantly? That was what it was designed for, after all.

Zukie made one last foray, and then, giving up on modern technology, she wrote down a number and went to the phone.

A minute later, she was jiggling Joe so he wouldn't cry at an inopportune moment, and putting on her most cultivated voice.

"I wonder if you could possibly help me," she said to the person who had the misfortune of answering her call. "I'm working with Shirley and I just need one small item of information."

"Shirley Carson?"

Zukie was stymied, but then she realized that Shirley probably wouldn't have wanted to use such a distinctive last name as Minghella, even if she was entitled to it, in connection with anything underhanded. So she decided to take a chance and forged ahead.

"Yes, that's right. Could you help me with that?"

"What do you need to know, ma'am?"

"I'm afraid I lost my notes that said who donated that wonderful *netsuke* collection to the museum. Could you remind me where they came from?"

"Just a minute, please."

Zukie held her breath, trying to hear either pages turning or a keyboard clicking. She hoped that the person she was speaking to was a receptionist and not totally *au fait* with the exhibits. Otherwise, she could legitimately demand to know why Zukie didn't already have the answer to her question.

"They weren't donated, only loaned for a temporary exhibit a few months ago," said the voice. "It's closed now. There were two collections, but the main one was loaned by Clement Innes."

"Yes, of course," Zukie said, exhaling in relief. "I remember now. Thank you so much. Bye."

She hung up quickly and jotted down the name. Clement Innes. She pictured a tall, slightly stooped, white-haired gentleman who admired and collected Japanese antiques. He would be wealthy, of course, probably living in some mansion in one of the suburbs on the east side of Lake Washington.

He had loaned his prized collection to the museum, but somewhere along the line, someone had substituted a well-made modern replica for one or more of the genuine articles. And where were the real antiques now? Long gone, Zukie suspected, sold for a great deal of money on some art black market.

She was very pleased with this theory, even though it didn't explain Shirley's role. The police could fill in the details – that was what they were being paid for. Nor did it explain Shirley's death, but Zukie reasoned she couldn't be expected to do everything.

She was still preening herself when she heard the key turn in the front door and Lou came in.

"Hiya," she said cheerfully. "You've got some mail, but you probably shouldn't touch it."

LOU STOOD and gawked at her for a minute, wondering if his cousin was even more of a fruitcake than he had always suspected.

"Say what?"

"You have a postcard from Shirley."

"Very funny."

"I'm not joking, Lou. It's in the kitchen."

Lou brushed past her without a word and went into the kitchen. He came back holding the bag with the card inside.

"Is this some kind of sick joke, Zukie?"

"How could it be? I never saw it before."

"And if Shirley did send it, what the hell is she talking about? She never told me to remember anything."

"Nothing?" Zukie put a calculated amount of innuendo into her question and wasn't surprised when Lou scowled.

"Nothing to do with the art museum, or anything like that. I don't know why she would send me this."

"If she's the one who sent it. I don't suppose you remember which postcards she bought at the museum?"

"No, I don't. I wasn't paying attention and I sure didn't expect her to send me one of them."

"I wonder if it *is* from her," Zukie said thoughtfully. "Here, let me take a look at something."

Lou handed the card over and Zukie peered through the

plastic bag.

"Postmarked two days ago. Jeez, the mail is getting slow."

"That's the day before she died," Lou said.

"It's the day before Vance came and told us she was dead," Zukie corrected him. "But OK, let's assume it came from her and she mailed it before she died. Hang on."

"What?"

"It isn't postmarked 'Seattle'."

"So where was it mailed?"

"Mercer Island."

"So she was on Mercer Island that day," Lou said. "Maybe she went shopping there. Maybe she stuck it in a mail box while she was there. What's up with you?"

Zukie was staring at the card, and remembering her mental image of the collector who had loaned his items to the museum. She'd placed him in a wealthy east side suburb, a description which could fit Mercer Island. The island in the middle of Lake Washington was home to some extremely wealthy people, even if it was only half way to the east side of the lake.

"I'd sure like to know," she said, "where a guy called Clement Innes lives."

Chapter 12

"OK, I'll bite," Lou said. "Who is Clement ... what's the name?"

"Clement Innes."

"Who the heck is he?"

"He's a guy who loaned his real nice collection of valuable antique *netsuke* to the art museum. Not a permanent exhibit, just a temporary one a few months ago. But long enough, I guess, for them to put a picture of it on a postcard. And long enough ..."

"For something fishy to happen to it," Lou said. "No pun intended, by the way."

"Exactly."

"I know I'm going to regret asking, but how did you find all this out, Zuke?"

"I phoned the art museum," Zukie said, surprised he had to ask such an obvious question. "OK, I looked on the computer first, but I couldn't find anything about it, so I just called them. The lady I talked to was real helpful."

"I hope you didn't say who you were."

"Of course not."

"Well, that's something."

Lou looked at the postcard again. "I suppose I'm going to have to give this to Vance and hope he can make some sense out of it."

"I have a better idea."

"Heaven help us. What is it?"

"Let's give it to Jim."

It only took Lou a second or two to follow her thinking, possibly a record time.

"You want to grill him."

"Why not? I'm tired of all these silly hints and half-truths Vance and Holt are telling us. If you – we – are in this thing up to our necks, we need to know what's really happening."

"Are we in it?"

"You're not driving a loaner because you got tired of your car, Lou."

"Yeah. I see what you mean. But Vance probably told Jim not to tell us anything."

Zukie conceded this was a possibility, in fact, a probability. Vance had a good track record when it came to keeping her out of the loop, even though she usually managed to slip in somehow.

"I know that, but it's worth a shot. If you'll keep an eye on Joe, I'll make a lemon meringue pie."

"Oh, that's sneaky, Zuke."

"Desperate times call for desperate measures, Lou. If there's some left, you can have a piece. Here, Joe, you can play with Uncle Lou for a while."

Zukie handed Joe over and went into the kitchen. She didn't consider it underhanded to bake her son-in-law's favorite dessert as a sort of bribe – *incentive*, she quickly corrected herself – to get him to open up. She found herself wondering if she had even had this plan in her subconscious when she had picked out the lemons at the supermarket.

No, the challenge would be to get Lanigan on his own, fill him with pie and then extract any information he could provide. No sweat, she assured herself.

She mixed up the dough for the crust, shaping it into a neat ball and popping it into the fridge to chill while she got out the ingredients for the lemon filling and the meringue topping. Lemon meringue pie was one of her specialties and she could almost make it with her eyes closed, but this one was serving a special purpose, so it had to be perfect.

Noises from the living room told her that Lou and Joe were spending some quality time together; Lou making lion growling sounds and Joe squealing happily in response. Zukie was thankful Lou had five young grandchildren of his own, since she knew some men of his age would have totally panicked at being asked to amuse a baby for half an hour. But Lou seemed to be enjoying the game almost as much as Joe was.

She rolled out the chilled dough, fitted it into the pie dish and put it in the oven to be pre-baked just long enough to keep the filling from soaking into it. While it was baking, she heated the lemon filling in a saucepan and beat egg whites and sugar into a frothy mixture.

It all came together – the pre-baked crust, the hot lemon filling and the meringue, and she slid the pan into the oven for a final session, just enough to lightly brown the snowy peaks of meringue. When it was in, she picked up the kitchen phone and called Lanigan's number.

"Hey, Jim," she said. "I had some extra lemons, so I made a lemon meringue pie this afternoon. If you want to drop by when you're free, I'll save you a piece."

"That's nice of you, Zukie," Lanigan said, trying not to drool. "And as it happens, that will work out fine, because Carol's got a couple of late calls to make, so she said she might not be able to get there until later. So I'll drop by for some pie and take Joe back with me."

"Oh, I don't mind having Joe a little longer," Zukie said. "But I think he likes to get back to mommy and daddy."

"So I'll come by about six-thirty unless something comes up."

"That's great. I'll make sure Lou doesn't eat all the pie first. See you later."

"Bye, Zukie."

She hung up the phone and punched the air gleefully. It wasn't often that one of her plans went without a hitch, and even if for some reason Lanigan got delayed or backed out altogether, there would be a delicious lemon meringue pie to console her.

"Win-win situation," Zukie said, and took the pie out of the oven.

BY THE time Lanigan rang the doorbell, Zukie was primed for action. She had served Lou one of her never-fail dinners, consisting of fried chicken and spaghetti, with a crisp green salad on the side, and coached him on what to say to Lanigan. More importantly, she had reminded him of what he shouldn't say, and after a few grumbles, he had agreed.

Joe had joined them for dinner, sitting in his high chair and gumming a baby biscuit while the adults ate their meal. Then Zukie fed him some more cereal and a yogurt and Lou washed the dishes. She mopped Joe off, prepared a bottle of milk and took him into the bedroom, reasoning that if his mouth was occupied, it would be easier to converse without interruption. If they were lucky, he might even go to sleep first.

Promptly on the stroke of six-thirty, the bell rang and Lou went to answer it.

"I can smell that pie from here," Lanigan said, grinning. "In fact, I could swear I could smell it over the phone when Zukie called me."

Joe had been nearly asleep, but came awake with a start on hearing his father's voice.

"Damn," Zukie muttered. She forced herself to sound cheerful and called, "Hi, Jim. Be with you in a minute."

"No hurry."

She could hear Lanigan and Lou discussing baseball while they waited for Joe to finish his bottle. Then she carried him into the living room and parked him on the sofa beside Lanigan.

"I'll get us all a piece of pie," she said. "All of us except the little guy, that is."

"Give him time," Lanigan said, giving his son a fond glance. "Another couple of years and he'll be chowing down like everyone else."

Zukie went to the kitchen and cut three pieces of pie, bringing them back to the living room and handing them around.

For a while there was silence, broken finally by Lanigan's appreciative, "This is fantastic, Zukie. So much better than the store-bought ones."

"If Carol gives you store-bought pies, I'll disown her," Zukie said. "Want another piece?"

"If you insist."

Zukie cut him a second piece and waited patiently while he ate it. Then she whisked his plate away and came back to sit down opposite him.

"We need some information, Jim," she said. "And don't think it's a one-way street. Lou's got something to show you that I think you'll find interesting, but before he does, tell us what happened to Shirley."

Lanigan nodded. "I assumed you were trying to bribe me," he said. "Lemon meringue pie doesn't just fall into my lap like this without a reason."

"I wanted to make sure you were in a good mood," Zukie said. "You can call it a bribe if you want to. What happened to Shirley?"

"She's dead, Zukie."

"I know that. How? When? Where?"

Lanigan eyed his mother-in-law. "I could ask why you need to know."

"Because Lou and I need to know what we're dealing with."

"You're not in any danger."

"Danger of what? Lou being arrested for murder? Or one of us being the next target?"

They locked gazes. Lanigan sighed and said, "She died early yesterday morning. One gunshot wound, probably a handgun."

"Where was she?"

"In her home."

"Which I bet isn't in Georgetown, no matter what she told Lou."

"No, it isn't."

"On Mercer Island? No, I guess it wouldn't be, 'cause then it wouldn't be you Seattle guys investigating it."

"Why did you say Mercer Island?" Lanigan asked.

"Just a thought."

"I hate it when you have thoughts," Lou muttered.

"Why Mercer Island?" Lanigan repeated.

Zukie tried to look innocent, which was always difficult. It hadn't worked in grade school, when the nuns always knew she was the one causing trouble. It hadn't worked with her parents, either, no matter how hard she'd tried to shift the blame onto Angela.

She said, "Well, that kind of brings us to the other half of why you're here, Jim. I admit you haven't been too helpful, but at least we know a little more than we did. Who found her?"

"Not relevant."

"Jim," Zukie said. "You are the father of my grandson, but I'm going to clobber you one if you don't answer my question."

"She lived long enough to press the emergency button on her security system. So the police responded and found her. She was taken to Harborview but she didn't make it. Happy now?"

"Not really. You guys didn't give Lou and me any emergency button to press. And if she had a security system, how'd the shooter get inside?"

"They didn't. The shot came through a window."

Zukie involuntarily glanced at her windows and vowed not to go anywhere near them until Shirley's killer was caught.

"All right, what's the other half?" Lanigan asked. "Does it have something to do with Mercer Island?"

Zukie looked at Lou.

"I got something in the mail today," he said. "Supposedly it came from Shirley, but I won't swear to that."

"Let's see it."

Lou went into the kitchen and came back with the postcard. He handed it silently to Lanigan, who looked at the picture, then turned it over.

"Is that her handwriting, Lou?"

"I don't know. I never saw anything she wrote."

"So you don't know whether she sent it."

"Wouldn't you guys have something she wrote, if she was working with you?" Zukie asked. "Then you could compare it."

Lanigan shifted uneasily. "I'm not aware of her writing anything. Mostly verbal contact, I'd think."

"But you could ask."

"I could. What's this message supposed to mean, Lou?"

"I don't know."

"You sure about that?"

"Yes."

"I wonder how she happened to choose this particular postcard. Did you know why?"

"No."

"You're playing your cards awfully close to your chest all of a sudden," Lanigan said easily. "Where did the postcard come from? It looks like the art museum."

"Probably was, then."

"Did you go there with her?"

That was the question Zukie had hoped Lanigan wouldn't ask, but she supposed it was inevitable that sooner or later it would be.

"Yeah. Once."

"And did she buy the card then?"

"I think so."

"More than one card?"

"A couple."

"So she might have sent the other one to someone else."

"She might have just kept it," Zukie said. "When Lou and me went to Italy, I bought a load of postcards, but I didn't send them all. I kept some just to look at, to remind me of where we'd been. Pictures don't always come out the way you want them to, or there's somebody in the way or something."

"True enough." Lanigan remembered receiving an enthusiastic postcard when Zukie and Lou had gone on a whirlwind tour of the Old Country. He reckoned that more than a year later, Italy might have recovered from the experience.

"And since she's dead, I don't imagine Lou will be getting any more mail from her."

"Right again. Lou, I'll take this with me and see if forensics can get anything off it."

"Don't hold your breath," Zukie said. "The mailman would have touched it and heaven knows how many other people along the way."

"I know that, but we can try. Thank you for telling me about it. Is there anything else you're holding back?"

"Nope. How about you?"

Lanigan smiled. "Zukie, SPD is not obliged to provide you with every detail of an on-going homicide investigation."

"I know that. Jeez, you've told me enough times. Have you gotten any further? How about that plastics place?"

"We'll check it out."

"And you'll be going to Mercer Island."

"Yes, we ... why?"

"The postcard was mailed from there," Zukie said, aiming again for total innocence. "Of course, there might be some other reason."

"Don't let your imagination go into overdrive, Zukie," Lanigan warned. "And please, leave the investigation to us."

"Sure. That's what we pay our taxes for. I'll just get Joe's stuff."

She went into the bedroom to get the bag of baby paraphernalia, guessing that Lanigan and Lou were exchanging non-verbal opinions of her. That was all right; she'd at least learned something new from the visit.

She carried the bag out and gave Joe a last cuddle and kiss.

"I'll see you next week, sweetie."

"Thanks for having him, Zukie. We do appreciate it. And thanks for the pie, too."

"Any time."

Zukie watched from the doorway as Lanigan loaded Joe and the bag into his car. She waved as they drove off and then turned to Lou.

"That went all right, didn't it?"

"I guess. I wish I knew what this was all about."

"We'll find out somehow, Lou. In the meantime, I think we better stay back from the windows."

"I wonder if that was true, her being shot through a window."

Zukie frowned at him, since being skeptical of information provided by the police or other authorities was usually her area of expertise.

"Why wouldn't it be?"

"To scare you off, I'd guess."

"Oh, for heaven's sake." Zukie glanced at the window. "Still, it won't do any harm to be careful."

LANIGAN drove back to his own house, and carried Joe inside. He gave Carol a kiss and then went back out and drove to the precinct. Vance was waiting for him.

"Well?"

"An interesting development," Lanigan said. He handed the postcard to Vance. "This came in today's mail for Mr Romano."

Vance perused both sides of the postcard. "And I suppose he has no idea what this refers to."

"He says not. And Lou's a pretty honest guy."

"Who seems to have gotten himself mixed up in something shady. Extremely shady."

"He tells me he and Shirley went to the art museum one day and she bought a couple of cards in their gift shop. Presumably this is one of them. But that's all he could say about it. He doesn't know what the message means."

Vance pointed to one of the *netsuke* in the photograph.

"This is the one he found, isn't it? The fish."

"Yes. So there may be a message of some sort there. My next question would be: Is the one in the photo the real one or the fake? And how about the others? How many fake ones are there?"

Vance nodded. "*My* next question would be: If they're fake, did people at the museum know they were exhibiting chunks of modern plastic? They must have experts there who should have been able to tell. And if they were displaying the real stuff, who did the switch and when? Lanigan, I sometimes wish I were back on traffic patrol. It's a hell of a lot more straightforward than chasing art thieves who may or may not have shot a woman who was supposed to be working with SPD."

Lanigan correctly deduced he wasn't supposed to answer any of those questions. Vance laid the postcard on his desk.

"Another item for the file. I'll have forensics check and see if this is actually her handwriting. And if Mr Romano gets any more mail from beyond the grave, I hope you told him to notify us."

"Yes, I did."

"Did you enjoy your pie?"

Lanigan grinned. "Very much. Two pieces. As Detective Graham once described it, heaven on a plate."

"At least you got that much out of your session. Did you manage to get anything else from your mother-in-law and Mr Romano? After all, that's the reason I sent you over there."

Chapter 13

"Not too much," Lanigan said regretfully. "Although I must admit it was real handy, her asking me to drop by for a piece of pie at the same time you wanted me to grill her and Lou, so I didn't have to dream up an excuse. I'll put that down to coincidence."

"Let's hope that's all it was. I don't trust her."

"She did manage to slip Mercer Island into the conversation, but that could be because the postcard was mailed from there. I can't think of any other reason."

"She didn't mention Clement Innes?"

"No. She asked how Shirley died and I said she was shot through a window of her house."

"Well, at least part of that was true," Vance said. "You didn't give her any other details, did you?"

"No, of course not."

"Good. Maybe that will be enough to keep her from getting too closely involved."

"That was before Zukie told me about the postcard. She asked if Shirley lived on Mercer Island, because she's worked out she didn't live in Georgetown."

"How did she know that?" Vance asked, frowning.

"Probably because her sister would have known her, or known something about her, if she had. Angela lives in Mount Baker, but she has long tentacles."

Vance looked as though he either wanted to bang his head on the desk or phone Angela and offer her a job. He opted for neither.

"On the other hand, we have to ask ourselves what Shirley was doing hanging around that part of town, and you can bet it had something to do with that plastics business. Checking them out is going to be the next job on the list, Lanigan. Someone had to make those very good copies, and what better place than somewhere that makes molded plastic stuff?"

"CHECKING out Minghella Plastics is the next thing to do," Zukie said firmly.

"Count me out, Zuke. I've had enough of all this."

"You're such a wimp, Lou."

Lou glowered at her. "So what are you planning to do? March in there and ask if they happened to have done a job for someone that involves making real good copies of antique doo-dahs so they look like old ivory? Maybe even good enough to display at a museum?"

"Of course not. And anyway, it might have been the real ones that went on display. The people at the museum would know if they were was fakes."

"And if these are the same people who shot Shirley, they aren't playing games."

"I know that, too. I'll think of something."

"Zukie, just drop it. Please."

Zukie looked at him in surprise. It was unlike Lou to plead with her, since blustering was more his usual style. She wondered if he was genuinely worried about her safety or whether he was just concerned that he'd have to cook for himself if anything happened to her.

"Lou, I'm not planning to do anything stupid."

"Fine. Trouble is, your definition of stupid doesn't match anyone else's. Drop it."

"Tell you what, Lou. I'll give it a couple of days and if the police find out what's going on and nab Shirley's killer, then there won't be any reason for me to do anything. OK?"

"It's better than nothing, I guess."

"Good. Let's watch a DVD now."

She deliberately let Lou choose what they would watch, knowing he would pick a war film or a Western, and since she wasn't very interested in either of those, she could let her mind wander down more productive paths while she pretended to watch.

Sure enough, five minutes later they were watching an action-packed film set during World War II. Zukie already knew who had won, so she thought about Shirley, Minghella Plastics and the as yet mysterious Clement Innes.

She doubted Mr Innes would be listed in the phone book or anywhere else that would make him easy to locate. Someone wealthy enough to afford a collection of valuable antiques would not want to advertise his presence.

Nor did she remember ever hearing his name in connection with any local businesses or activities. There was, of course, the possibility that he wasn't from the Seattle area, in which case she might as well give up.

But the way Lanigan had pounced on her mention of Mercer Island led Zukie to think some of the answers might lie at the other end of the floating bridge over Lake Washington, and it seemed a likely place for a rich collector to live. Therefore there had to be a way of finding out more about Innes, either to tie him in or rule him out.

"That's the key," she said aloud.

Lou shot her an irritated glance. "I know. I've seen it before."

"I wasn't talking about the movie."

"Saints preserve us. Now what?"

"Just thinking. Watch the movie, Lou."

He turned back to the screen and Zukie returned to her thoughts. By eliminating the fancy touches, it boiled down to a simple narrative, or so she imagined. Clement Innes had loaned his collection of valuable antique *netsuke* to the museum for a temporary exhibit. Somewhere along the line, either before the exhibit has closed, or more likely afterwards, the *netsuke* had been switched, with the expert reproductions replacing the originals.

Innes had realized his collection had been stolen and had alerted the police. They had subsequently recruited a woman who was an expert on Oriental art to help them track down the thieves, the *netsuke* or both. Someone didn't like that idea and had shot her.

So far, so good. Or, Zukie realized, she could be completely on the wrong track. That was what came of theorizing without evidence, something no fictional detective would do.

All right, she said to herself. *Back up and start again.*

The fake items had probably originated at Minghella Plastics. Shirley, who was using that last name whether or not she was entitled to, was involved up to her neck. Either she had known all along about the fakes and was possibly even responsible for them, or she had just realized what was going on and was intending to expose the racket.

It could be, Zukie mused, that the *netsuke* weren't the only objects that had been stolen and replaced by reproductions, but only the most recent or most prominent ones. There might have been any number of things made of ivory or bone or something else that could be replicated in high quality plastic and finished off by a competent artist. Innes might not have been the only victim.

The big question, the one that she couldn't find a plausible answer for, was why Lou had been dragged into whatever crime had been committed. It was just possible that Shirley had initially been attracted by her cousin's pleasant demeanor and helpfulness, but why involve a law-abiding retired plumber in some underhanded, illegal activity?

She looked at Lou, absorbed in the war movie, and realized she had just answered her own question. It was because Lou *was* an ordinary person with no criminal record that he had been roped in. The police would have no reason to connect him with the theft of valuable antiques. And if Shirley had realized Lou's second cousin was on a first-name basis with several police officers, she might have picked some other innocent accomplice.

Zukie, who had been feeling somewhat sympathetic toward Shirley, now felt only anger. How dare that woman drop Lou into a dangerous situation just to protect herself? He could have been seriously injured or even killed in the parking garage incident, and she had a feeling he wasn't out of the woods yet.

Of course, Shirley herself had paid the ultimate price, but that didn't make Zukie feel much better about the whole affair. At least, she thought wryly, Lou would think twice before ever offering to help a stranded driver again, even a good-looking one.

The main problem at the moment, as she saw it, was that although the police didn't seem to think Lou was guilty of anything except possibly poor judgement, the thieves didn't hold the same opinion. Hence the destruction of his car seats, whether intended as a warning or because they genuinely expected to find something hidden there.

A burst of gunfire made her jump and then look at the screen, where a major battle was taking place. Zukie took this as a sign the movie was winding to a close and brought her attention back to the present.

"Hey, I should have made some popcorn to eat while we were watching," she said.

"Too late now. Besides, it's not a popcorn type of movie."

"What kind is that?"

"Something light and fluffy. A comedy, maybe."

Zukie decided not to argue. The final credits rolled and Lou took the DVD out of the player and put the case back on the shelf.

"I'm having an early night, Zuke. This whole thing is getting to me."

He did look tired and Zukie felt a rare wave of sympathy. Never mind that he had brought it on himself; he hadn't asked for anything this serious.

"OK. I won't be late, either."

Lou wandered off in the direction of the bathroom and Zukie went into the kitchen. She paced the floor for a minute or so, then picked up the phone.

"Hey, Ange."

"What is it?"

"You find out anything about the Minghellas and that company?"

"Not much," Angela said regretfully. "Ray says the company makes molded plastics. I'm not sure what that means."

"I do."

"You do?"

"Yeah. Go on."

"They've been in business quite a while and have a good reputation."

"Does the family run it?"

Zukie's on-line research hadn't revealed any information about who the key players were, which seemed like either a major oversight on their part or an attempt to hide something. She was opting for the latter.

"I really don't know, Zukie. I know you asked me about Mike Minghella, but I don't know anybody with that name."

"Did you ask …"

"And I asked around, too. So I can't give you any more information."

"Yet."

"OK. You haven't ever heard of a guy called Clement Innes, have you?"

She didn't expect a positive response to that and she didn't get one.

"Clement Innes? Never heard of him."

"Damn. OK."

"Zukie, I don't know everyone. There's a limit to what I can find out, you know."

"I never thought I'd hear you say that, Ange. Keep digging. Something will turn up."

She put the phone down on Angela's protests. She could hear Lou moving around in his bedroom, which meant the bathroom was free for her to have a long soak in a bubble bath and do a little more thinking.

As she ran the water, Zukie decided that in the morning, she would start trying to find out more about Clement Innes. This wasn't anything Angela could help with, since as far as she knew, the man didn't live in south Seattle, and her vast network did have its limitations.

So she sank into the bubbles, plotting a way to find someone who, under the circumstances, probably didn't want to be found.

VANCE and Holt stood in the middle of a living room, larger and more luxuriously furnished than Zukie's ever would be. It was nearly dark outside, and Vance switched on the ceiling lights so they could see the room clearly.

The furniture was a tasteful blend of wood and leather, sitting on polished wooden floorboards. A floor to ceiling set of shelves displayed books, CDs, DVDs and, of most interest to the pair, a collection of items which appeared to be Oriental antiques.

"No *netsuke*," Holt observed, scanning the shelves. "But this stuff here must be worth quite a bit of money. This looks like jade, and I think these are ivory."

"If they're real," Vance said drily. "OK, forensics have been through this already, so we don't have to be too concerned about disturbing evidence. But we'll still be careful."

Holt produced a camera and began photographing the items on the shelves. Vance read the titles of the books, which included several reference works on Asian art and antiques. He pulled a couple out and flipped through the pages, then shook them to see if anything fell out.

"I'll leave you to get on with this room," he said, replacing the books. "Check the rest of these books, will you? And the CDs and DVDs, too. I'll take a look at the bedroom."

He stood in the doorway first, letting his eyes rove around the room. It was furnished in a simple style and monochromatic color scheme, which in Vance's opinion, also reflected an Oriental influence. He told himself not to leap to conclusions, and went to look through the closet and chest of drawers.

The closet held a variety of clothes, most of them stylish and even to Vance's masculine eye, expensive. All the clothes were women's and all the same size, so it appeared Shirley hadn't shared her bedroom – or at least not her closet – with anyone. Vance pulled the hangers apart and looked at the back of the closet, tapping it to see if there were any concealed panels, but drew a blank.

The chest of drawers was equally innocent, holding underwear and neatly folded sweaters. Vance pulled each drawer out, removed the contents and examined the undersides, finding only wood. He replaced the contents, slid the drawers into place and moved to the bedside table.

This held a lamp, a box of tissues and a water glass. Vance bent over and pulled out the small drawer under the top, which held two pens, a small notebook with blank pages, a tube of hand lotion and some lip salve.

He looked a little more closely at the notebook, where the first two or three pages had been torn from the binding, and his eyes narrowed. He closed the drawer and went back into the living room.

"Any luck, Holt?"

"Not yet. I'll take a look at her desk next. Was there anything of interest in the bedroom?"

"It appears the paper found on her came from a small notebook in the bedside table. Otherwise, no. It looks like a hotel room, very neat and impersonal. Of course, we know she hadn't lived here very long."

"Six months, wasn't it, since she came back from Japan?"

"About that. Let's look at the desk. Forensics has her laptop, but there may be something else."

The desk was basically a table with a shelf above it and a filing cabinet at one end with a printer on it. Vance opened the top drawer of the filing cabinet and began to leaf methodically through the files. It didn't take long.

"There is very little here of a personal nature," he said after a few minutes. "A few documents and paperwork, but I think she probably did most things on-line, and if she did, the IT guys will track it down. There's no personal correspondence, photographs or anything like that."

"Nothing from SPD?" Holt asked.

"No. Nothing in writing."

"Prudent of her. And no postcards?"

Vance paused. "Good point, Holt. She sent the one to Romano, but he said she bought more than one. So either they should be here or, God help us, she sent them to someone else, who may or may not be kind enough to notify us."

"She could have had it on her, couldn't she? The shooter took her purse and phone."

"Yes. I think they were disturbed, or they would have searched her more thoroughly and found that note that led us to Romano. Damn."

Holt nodded and said, "Shall I check the kitchen?"

"Yes. I'll give you a hand."

They went into the small kitchen. Zukie, had she been there, would have been disgusted at the small amount of both cooking utensils and food. Shirley might have told Lou she liked to cook, but there was little evidence of it here.

Vance looked into the fridge, finding only a half empty carton of milk, a few pieces of fruit, a cube of butter, and four eggs. He opened the freezer and took out the ice cube trays, squinting into them.

"Anything there?" Holt asked.

"No. I once found a nice haul of diamonds frozen into some ice cubes, but this is just ice, I'm afraid. Real ice, that is. Start checking the cupboards and I'll look in the oven."

But the oven was bare. Holt took boxes and cans out of the cupboards and emptied canisters of coffee, sugar and rice into bowls. Vance upended jars of herbs and spices. Neither found anything but the original contents.

Vance grimaced. "She was careful, I'll give her that. This condo could have belonged to just about anyone. OK, there's an Asian influence, but in the Seattle area, that's not unusual, and given her history, it's even less surprising. What we're missing are any personal touches."

They went back into the living room and Holt indicated one of the windows, boarded up over a starburst of broken glass.

"You could call that a personal touch, I suppose."

"So you could." Vance's cell phone rang, and he held it to his ear. His expression, never very jovial, hardened into one of irritated disbelief. He closed his eyes for a second, as if to marshal his thoughts, or possibly to pretend he had imagined the phone call.

"Right, we'll head back across the bridge. Thanks."

He looked at Holt.

"We're done here, I think. And we now have something else to deal with."

ZUKIE pulled the plug from the bathtub drain and stood up, reaching for her fluffy pink towel. Lou had been campaigning since he moved in for a less pink bathroom, but Zukie liked it. She had been something of a tomboy in her childhood, scorning anything that was even remotely pink, but over the years, she had decided it was a good color for bathrooms and bedrooms. Eddie had never complained – come to think about it, she hadn't given him a choice – so she saw no reason why Lou should.

Once dry, she put on a nightgown decorated with pink flowers, and a pink terrycloth bathrobe. Her feet went into fluffy pink slippers. She padded around the house making sure everything was locked, set the alarm the way she'd been shown, and then settled herself in bed, pulling a pink flowered bedspread up over her.

Zukie was nearly asleep when the first noise came, a scratching sound that jolted her into full wakefulness. She sat up in bed, listening. It sounded as though someone was trying to force the lock on the front door and Zukie cursed the fact that she had left her purse in the kitchen. She didn't have a phone in the bedroom and she frankly lacked confidence in the police assurance that they would respond to any intrusion within minutes. She didn't have minutes anyway; she had seconds, and she could hear Lou snoring.

That meant it was up to her to stop whoever was trying to get in.

Zukie slipped out of bed, unplugged her bedside lamp and picked it up. She eased the bedroom door open a crack, holding the lamp over her head. She had scared a would-be burglar off this way once before, so she hoped it would work again.

She threw the bedroom door wide open and just as the alarm went off, she began to scream at the top of her lungs.

Chapter 14

By the time Vance and Holt arrived at Zukie's house, a patrol car had already pulled up, along with another unmarked police vehicle. Next door, Matt and Shelly were on their front porch, wide-eyed, and various other lights and twitching curtains showed the rest of the neighborhood was also aware that Zukie Merlino had somehow gotten herself involved in another police case.

Vance hurried down the walk to the front door. He had no great affection for Zukie, but he didn't want to have to explain to his superiors how someone supposedly being monitored by the police around the clock had been either burglarized or attacked.

So for once he was relieved to hear her voice in full flow, complaining that it had taken them long enough to get there and they were damn lucky she and Lou hadn't been murdered in their beds.

"You'd have a tough time explaining that one after you said you'd be watching all the time," she was saying, echoing Vance's own thoughts.

"All right, Mrs Merlino," he said, noting the look of relief that swept across the faces of the patrol car's occupants. Vance was here; let him deal with this nutcase. "Can you tell me what happened?"

"Someone tried to break in," Zukie said. "Pretty damn obvious, I'd say."

Vance took in the pink bathrobe, flowered nightgown and fluffy slippers.

"You'd already gone to bed?"

"Yes, we were both really tired. So we went to bed early, about nine-thirty or so."

Lou nodded. He was also in his pajamas and bathrobe and looked as one might expect a man to look who had been roused from a sound sleep by a security alarm and a screaming banshee.

"And then what happened?"

"I heard someone trying to get in the front door," Zukie said. "Trying to force the lock, I think. It wasn't long after I'd gone to bed, so maybe about ten. If someone was watching the house, they'd have seen the lights go out."

Vance mentally gave her credit for that observation, although he refused to give her any verbal encouragement.

"That's a little early for burglars," he said. "Your lights might have gone out, but most of your neighbors would still be up and would have seen or heard something. And as you say, it wasn't long after you retired, so they couldn't have expected you to be asleep yet."

Lou stirred a little at that. "You think they didn't care whether we heard them?"

"Or they were going to do something to us so it didn't matter whether we heard them or not," Zukie said darkly.

"I'm not sure what to think," Vance admitted. "I'm reasonably sure they didn't expect an alarm to go off, though."

"Yeah, it's pretty loud, I got to say. Scare anybody off. And would that camera have taken photos of them?" Zukie asked, pointing in the direction of the porch.

"Yes, the monitor at the precinct should show them."

"So what happens now? We go back to bed and wait for them to turn up again?"

It was a fair question, Vance had to admit.

"As pointless as it sounds, yes, that's probably the best thing to do. Go back to bed, that is. I doubt they'll come back after this."

He indicated the police presence, the flashing red and blue lights and Lou and Zukie, both in rumpled nightclothes but undeniably wide awake.

"And of course, we'll be checking the monitor to see what we can get off that."

"Gosh, that makes me feel so much better."

"Good," Vance said, ignoring the sarcasm. He turned to the patrol car pair. "Anything on the lock?"

"A couple of scratches where I think they were picking it," said one of the officers. He nodded toward the unmarked car, where two men were deep in conversation. "They dusted it, but no prints."

"Of course not," Zukie said. "These guys aren't amateurs, are they?"

"No."

"Do you know who they are? 'Cause I don't think it's just coincidence someone tried to break in here just after they trashed the upholstery in Lou's car."

"I agree, the two incidents are probably connected, but we haven't identified the perpetrators," Vance said.

"Well, you better find out," Zukie warned him. "I'm not going to sit up all night, every night, waiting to bash burglars."

Lou muttered something about almost feeling sorry for the burglars if she did.

Vance said, "We don't expect you to. We'll get back to the precinct and see what we can learn. We'll be in touch if needed."

"So you want me to stay up for a while?"

"No, we'll contact you tomorrow."

Zukie looked like she wanted to argue but Lou said, "All right. Thanks for coming out. Come on, Zuke."

He grasped her arm and propelled her back into the living room. Vance made a mental note that brute force seemed an effective technique in dealing with Mrs Merlino, although of course he was not a relative with more than half a century of experience in handling her.

"Good night," he said to her retreating back.

"Hmph," Zukie said.

Vance waited until he heard the door lock being engaged and the alarm being re-set, then joined Holt in their car.

"Precinct?" she asked.

"Yeah. This is getting way out of hand. Let's see what the monitor shows."

ZUKIE KNEW that the sensible course of action was the one Vance had suggested, which was why she instantly rejected it.

"I'm going back to bed," Lou said.

"Go ahead."

"Aren't you?"

"I'll stay up for a while. It's not that late, only about ten-thirty."

"Promise you won't attack anybody?"

"Lou, if someone breaks in here, you're darned right I'll attack them. This is my house – OK, mine and yours – and they've got no right to break in, especially when we haven't even got anything worth stealing."

"In that case, you might as well let them come in and find that out for themselves," Lou said. "You stay up if you want. I'm going to get some sleep, I hope."

He stalked off into his bedroom and closed the door firmly. Zukie glared at it for a moment and then went to get her purse from the kitchen. If there was a second attempt, she wanted to be better prepared than before, and besides the cell phone, she had more cash in her wallet than she wanted to lose to a crummy burglar.

She stopped in the living room on her way back through and picked up the wrought-iron fireplace poker. She took both items into her bedroom and propped herself up against the headboard of the bed, one hand on the phone and the other on the poker.

Five minutes later, she was asleep.

VANCE and Holt probably would have liked to get some sleep, too, but before they could, they were studying the images from the camera on Zukie's front porch.

Two figures were clearly visible, their faces partly obscured but enough features showing that Vance felt optimistic.

"We're going to feel foolish if this was just a random burglary attempt," he said, "but I don't think it was."

"Even if it was, we'd have a good chance of identifying them," Holt said. "But I agree."

Vance turned to the technician. "See if you can get a clear enough shot of both of them to run through the system," he said. "I don't think these guys are first-timers, so they should be on a database somewhere."

"Yes, sir."

"I'm heading home now. With luck, we'll have an ID by the time I get back."

THE SOUND of the poker falling on the floor woke Zukie, and for a moment she stared and wondered why it was in her bedroom. Then memory kicked in and she recalled the events of the night before.

Someone had tried to break into the house. She had repelled them single-handedly. OK, with a little help from the alarm system and the patrol car braking to a halt in front of the house. She dimly remembered two figures disappearing down the street as she opened the door, which in retrospect she felt might not have been the smartest course of action. A fireplace poker was all very well, but not much use against a gun, if they had brandished one at her.

She looked at the clock and realized there wasn't much point in going back to sleep, since she'd only have to get up again shortly. So, feeling a little sheepish, she climbed out of bed, got herself washed and dressed and went into the kitchen.

Two cups of coffee later, she had a plan, one that didn't involve any weapons except brainpower, and Zukie felt she was on a level footing with everyone else in that area. Perhaps even a little ahead, despite the opinions frequently expressed by Lou and her siblings.

She heard Lou moving around in his bedroom and reached for the frying pan. Eight minutes later, he was sitting down to French toast and a couple of nicely broiled sausages, and Zukie was putting the finishing touches on her idea, wondering why she always thought more coherently when she was around food.

"What you doing today, Lou?" she asked him.

"Not much. I've got a model I want to finish up and I might go out to lunch with Dave and Neal. That OK with you?"

"Sure. Sounds like a plan. I know you haven't had much time to work on your models lately."

Lou glared over the top of his coffee cup. "You mean when I was going out with Shirley."

"You said it, not me."

"And what are *you* doing today, Mother Theresa?"

"Oh, I might go see Angela. I haven't been over for a while."

"You're lying, Zuke. What are you really doing?"

Zukie decided not to dignify that with an answer, although it was annoying that Lou had caught her in a lie. It had been bad enough that Lanigan was suspicious of her motives, but she didn't have to share a house with him.

"Oh, stop worrying," she said. "I'm not doing anything wrong."

"Probably depends on how you define 'wrong'," Lou said. "But I'll pretend I believe you."

She gave him a warm smile and re-filled his coffee cup. Irritating as he could be, especially when he was right, she needed him on her side.

After he had finished and taken the breakfast dishes to the sink to wash, Zukie retreated to her bedroom to put the finishing touches on her plan. For one thing, she needed to get a wig, since being recognized wasn't part of the plan, and she was all too aware of her usual dishevelled appearance. So she settled her favorite auburn wig over her hair and looked at her reflection in the mirror with satisfaction.

She went back into the kitchen and said, "Lou, can I use your laptop for a few minutes?"

"Why?"

Zukie rolled her eyes at the ceiling. "To look something up. It won't take long."

"If you must."

"Jeez, Lou, it's not like I'm going to break it or anything. I know what I'm doing now."

"That's what worries me. Yeah, go ahead."

"Thanks."

She went into Lou's bedroom, shaking her head at the sight of the rumpled bedclothes. Zukie always re-made her own bed the minute she got out of it, the result of years of her Ma's training, but Lou's mother had obviously skipped this part. Sometimes Zukie made his bed, just because an unmade bed annoyed her, and sometimes she left it.

This time she decided to ignore it and sat at Lou's desk. A few minutes on the laptop confirmed her suspicion of the previous evening and she glared at the screen before remembering she had promised Lou she wouldn't damage his laptop. She needed information the internet couldn't provide and her target was well beyond even Angela's reach. It was exasperating.

With a sigh, she closed down the laptop and went back into the kitchen. Lou had finished the dishes and started to spread the model parts out on the table, so she assumed he would be occupied for a while.

"OK, I'm off," she told him. "I should be back by lunch time."

Lou cast an eye at the wig, but for once refrained from comment. "I may not be here, if I go to lunch with the guys. We might even get a game or two in, if there's a lane free."

"In that case, I'll see you when I see you. Bye."

"Bye."

Zukie backed her car out of the driveway and set off down the hill. She wasn't exactly sure where she was going and since she refused to use a GPS on the grounds that she had lived in Seattle all her life and knew the roads better than a machine did, her route was a little haphazard.

But eventually she glimpsed the sign that said Minghella Plastics, and parked down the street from the building. The red and white sign told her she wasn't allowed to park there, but Zukie reckoned she'd only be a few minutes, so it wasn't likely she would get a ticket.

"OK, now what?" she said to herself. "You're here, but you can't just walk in and ask if they've made some fake Japanese antiques, can you?"

For a moment, she wished she had brought Shelly with her, since a good-looking thirty-something blonde was sure to get a better response than a dumpy almost-sixty woman, even with the auburn wig working to her advantage.

But Shelly wasn't there, so she had to think up something on her own. Would a plastics factory be selling anything, so she could pretend to be a customer? It looked depressingly industrial, so she doubted that tactic would work.

Eventually she decided that sitting in the car wouldn't help anything, so she got out and strolled toward the building. There was nothing sinister or even interesting about it, she decided, just what appeared to be an office area facing the street, and the bulkier building behind it which was probably where the plastic was molded. Or whatever they did to it. She didn't stop, just kept walking until she was well past Minghella Plastics, then did a casual about-face and started back again.

An old man smelling of beer and wearing a collection of cast-off clothing sidled up to her.

"Got a dollar, lady?"

Zukie sighed. She didn't like panhandlers, but at least he'd been reasonably polite. She dug a dollar bill from her purse and handed it to him.

"Thanks, ma'am."

"You're welcome. Now get lost; I don't need a wino

following me."

He grinned and ambled off. Zukie resumed her walk. This time, she slowed down as she passed and ventured a glance at the office, hoping to see someone inside. But the angle of the windows made it difficult to see through and although she could make out some dim figures inside, she couldn't see them clearly.

Zukie decided to make one more pass at the building, then give up and try another tack. She was concentrating so hard on the front of the building that she failed to see the two men who had come out of a side door and were watching her walk up the street and back down again.

She also failed to hear footsteps behind her and only became aware of their presence when her arm was seized, cursing the fact that there were so many aggressive panhandlers around these days. At least the previous one had been courteous.

"Hey, let go of me," she snapped. "You want cash; I'll give you each a buck."

"We don't want your money," the man said. "You're Mrs Merlino, yeah?" His companion crowded in on the other side and Zukie's anger flared. She was so angry she didn't even stop to ask herself how they knew her name.

"What the hell do you think you're doing? I got a right to walk down the street, and if you don't let me go, I'm going to start screaming."

"Yeah, you're good at that," the man commented. His companion chuckled grimly.

"You tried to break into my house last night," Zukie said, with dawning awareness. She scowled at the man. "And you probably wrecked Lou's car, too. Why? We don't have whatever it is you're looking for. So shove off and leave us alone."

She tried to yank her arm out of the man's grasp, but he was stronger than she was. With a jolt, Zukie suddenly realized that she could be in real danger, but she had never backed down from a fight in her life and she wasn't about to start now.

She kicked hard at his shin, drawing a curse, and tried to ram her elbow backward into his stomach. Unfortunately, her captor anticipated this move, and her elbow was immobilized as he hustled her along toward the building, the second man shielding her from being seen by anyone driving down the street.

Not that they would stop to help, Zukie thought sourly. It was an industrial part of the city, and the majority of vehicles were trucks and vans associated with the various businesses. *Well, you wanted to get inside Minghella Plastics and it looks like you're going to get your wish,* she thought.

But her captors took her past the door and around to the back of the building, where one of them slid the door of a van open.

"In," he said.

"No."

"God, you're stubborn, lady. Get in."

Zukie set her feet and refused to move. With a sigh, the man shoved his hands under her armpits, hoisted her up and tossed her onto the back seat of the van. As she struggled to get upright, he placed a cloth over her mouth and nose. Zukie gasped for breath, and then the world went black.

Chapter 15

About the same time Zukie was taking her unexpected trip, Vance was studying the information he'd been handed. One file concerned her nocturnal visitors, and another file contained background information on the art theft technique which had deprived several galleries and individuals of their collections.

"Those two who tried to get into Mrs Merlino's house," he said, tapping the top sheet of paper, "have a well-documented connection with Michael Minghella. What a surprise."

"Shirley's ex-husband?" Lanigan asked.

"Yes. He apparently has a taste for fine art, does Minghella, and specializes in the top end of the market. But he doesn't buy it or collect it; he steals it – or gets someone else to – and sells it to the highest bidder. Preferably small, portable items."

"Like the *netsuke*."

"That's right. Jewelry, small ceramics and as you say, things like antique snuffboxes and *netsuke*. Things you can literally fit in a pocket and walk off with. And his usual technique is to substitute a replica, something so close that the theft isn't noticed immediately."

"Which means," Holt said, "he or someone working with him has to be making excellent copies. And while the plastics company might turn up someone who could fake ivory or bone, I suppose they wouldn't be able to make a very convincing diamond necklace, or something like that."

"No," Vance said. "But I'm happy to let the art robbery guys work that one out. Our main concern is finding out what, if anything, Michael Minghella had to do with his ex-wife's death. He's been suspected in several thefts but was too slippery to ever get caught with the goods. If he can do that, he's smart enough to get someone else to snuff an ex-wife who was going to blow the whistle on him, if that's what she was going to do."

"I take it there's a definite connection between him and the plastics company," Lanigan said. "Do we think the fakes were made there?"

"His brother Steven owns and runs the company, apparently, so obviously Michael could get access to it. But we may find out that Michael was running his own show and that Steven and Minghella Plastics as a company had no idea what he was up to."

Lanigan remembered numerous occasions when Zukie had lectured him on the regrettable tendency of the general public to assume that all Italian-Americans had links to organized crime. She cited her own family's building firm, established in the 1920s and with an impeccable reputation for sound work and honesty, as an example.

At the time, Lanigan had been amused, but he had to admit she was right. And police officers knew better than to believe stereotypes; there were too many exceptions.

"That could well be true," he said. "Or there might be just one or two employees willing to be persuaded to help him out."

"Did Shirley ever work at the company?" Holt asked.

"No," Vance said. "At least not that anyone knows of. But she was married to the guy, so she must have been familiar with the business."

"At least the more honest aspects of it," Lanigan said. "When did the divorce take place?"

Vance had turned back to the report. "Almost ten years ago," he said. "Which begs the question, why did she wait until now to get involved in nailing him? She must have known what he was doing."

"Maybe she was taking a cut," Holt said.

"Maybe. Maybe not." Vance was frowning at the report. "So they were divorced and after a while, she apparently took off to travel the world, ending up in Japan before coming back here about six months ago. Is that a coincidence, I wonder?"

"That she was boning up on Japanese culture just before her ex was possibly stealing a collection of valuable Japanese antiques?" Lanigan said. "I wouldn't have thought so. Or maybe it's the other way around; he found out she knew about them and talked her into helping him."

"Either way, she was playing a very dicey game. So what the hell …" Vance's voice trailed off. "You'd have thought the art guys would have checked her out thoroughly before they agreed to use her as an adviser, but I'm beginning to wonder just how thorough they were."

ZUKIE CAME round with a jerk, literally, as the van hit a pothole. She felt nauseous, either from whatever had been on the cloth, or because she'd always been a martyr to travel sickness and being transported flat on the back seat of a van didn't help. She wondered what the reaction would be if she threw up on her captors. It would be too much to ask that they'd stop and throw her out of the vehicle.

Common sense told her to keep quiet and hope she might overhear something that would give her a clue as to where she was and where they were taking her. What they might do to her once they arrived was something she didn't really want to think about.

So she simply lay still, trying to look limp and unconscious. It must have worked, because she could hear someone talking on a cell phone and not seeming to worry that she could hear. Unfortunately, one side of the conversation was not too helpful, because the half she could hear consisted largely of monosyllabic responses.

She did gather, however, that the person on the other end of the call was not entirely happy about her presence.

"No, she's not," said the voice. And then, "I don't know."

She felt someone prod her arm, but with an effort, kept from reacting.

"Still out."

Zukie strained her ears, but couldn't hear the reply.

"OK. Five minutes."

A muted click told her the conversation was over. The same voice said, "He's not real happy about this."

"Can you blame him?" That must be the second man, who was driving. Good to know that criminals were obeying the law against using cell phones behind the wheel.

"Listen, it wasn't our fault. She was nothing but trouble."

"I know that."

"Maybe we shouldn't have snatched her," the first voice said. "But what the hell was she doing if not trying to blow the whole thing sky-high?"

Zukie lay there, eyes closed, listening and thinking. A sudden thought struck her and she almost yelped, but managed to keep both her eyes and mouth shut. The van slowed down, then stopped with the engine still running and she heard soft clicks, as if someone was keying in a code. She congratulated herself on working that out, because the next thing she heard was the sound of a gate sliding open and the van started up again.

There were no potholes on this road; it was smooth as glass. The van glided along for what felt like a mile or more, but was probably far less, before stopping. Zukie gulped, wondering what on earth would happen next. From the sound of it, they were on some kind of private estate, the sort where an inconvenient body could be dumped in the shrubbery and not discovered for years.

It was one of the few times in her life when she genuinely regretted not following someone else's advice or even her own common sense. *Oh, well*, she thought, *you got yourself into this, Susanna, and you'll have to get yourself out again.*

The van door slid open and cool air hit her face. Pretending that she had only just regained consciousness, Zukie opened her eyes cautiously.

"Where am I?" It seemed a reasonable question to ask. "I don't feel very well," she added truthfully.

The man who had originally grabbed her arm by the plastics company hauled her off the seat and stood her on her feet. Zukie let her legs buckle under her, not entirely on purpose.

"Stand up," he said sharply.

"I feel awful."

"You used too much," the driver told his companion. "Walk her around a little; get it out of her system."

That was fine with Zukie, who wanted to see as much as possible of her new location. She straightened her jacket and reached a hand for her head, surprised to find her wig was still there and more or less in place.

"It don't help," her captor advised her. "You still look like a wop."

The insult infuriated Zukie so much she forgot the circumstances and started her clenched fist for his jaw. He just chuckled and caught it before she reached him.

"Feisty, ain't you?"

"Shut up, jerk."

"Just walk her around, Len," the driver said wearily. "No good getting into a fight with her. You ought to have learned that by now."

Zukie perceived that the driver was marginally more intelligent than his companion, so she gave him a less hostile look as Len grasped her arm and pulled her along.

The van had stopped in a driveway beside a house. At least Zukie supposed it was a house, although in her opinion, several families could have fit into it and still had room left over. It was nestled against a hillside, with a small forest around it. On second glance, a tastefully landscaped forest, with rhododendrons, azaleas and other less recognizable shrubs dotted among the trees. A stone lantern stood in a clearing among the bushes.

The whole landscape looked slightly alien, but familiar at the same time, and after a moment she realized why. A few months earlier, she and Lou had visited the Japanese garden in the city's arboretum, and this had the same general appearance – extremely neat and tidy, with everything planted precisely where it would be shown to the best advantage, rotating with the seasons. Had she been in a better mood, she would have appreciated its beauty, but as it was, the landscaping might as well have been littered with weeds and rusty tin cans.

Len dragged her up and down the driveway until she said, "Jeez, Len, you've made your point. I can walk, OK? Let go of me."

"In your dreams."

"Listen, there's nowhere I can go, 'cause I don't have the faintest idea where we are. And you're probably faster than me, anyway."

Len thought that over, and then loosened his grip. Zukie rubbed her elbow.

"So where is this place?" she asked him.

Actually, she had a vague idea, having glimpsed water through the trees. She had managed to sneak a look at her wristwatch and given the time elapsed since she had been captured, she reckoned they hadn't driven very far.

So they were near a waterfront, most likely Lake Washington, and on someone's expensive private estate. She didn't think any of the well-known Seattle millionaires who had homes on the lakefront made a practice of kidnapping middle-aged widows, so it was someone else. Someone rich and unscrupulous, or at least someone rich who hired unscrupulous goons.

Len hadn't answered her, so she turned to the driver, who had lit a cigarette and was leaning against the van while Len walked her around.

"You any better at answering questions than your buddy is?"

"Nope," he said.

"Thanks."

"Any time." He stubbed out the cigarette, then carefully

picked up the butt and put it in the van's ashtray. "If she's better now, let's get her inside."

"Inside where?" Zukie asked, not expecting an answer. She didn't get one.

Len took her arm again and she resisted the impulse to hit him with her purse, which for some reason, was still over her other arm. Letting her keep it seemed rather careless of Len and his companion, so she filed away the idea that they weren't any better at kidnapping than they were at burglary.

He had a firm grip, however, and led her along a paved walk to a door. It was obviously not the main entrance, Zukie noted, but one used by less important people. The driver opened the door and Len gave her a shove which almost sent her sprawling inside.

Zukie straightened up and looked around her. Even if this was the servants' entrance, or something similar, it was fancier than anywhere she'd ever been. Or perhaps "fancy" wasn't the right word – "expensive" or "tasteful" would be more accurate.

Everything from the ceiling to the floor under her feet was simple, but the materials were of the highest quality. No plastic or vinyl here, but a variety of fine woods, tile and stone, harmoniously blended. Zukie wasn't the daughter and sister of professional builders for nothing, and she recognized that there was nothing second-rate about this place.

"Nice," she said. "Not your house, is it, Len?"

"Shut it."

"We're just the delivery service," the driver said.

"Yeah? Who ordered me?"

"Give it a rest," Len told her. "Nobody likes a smart ass."

Since Zukie had been making wisecracks mostly to lift her own spirits, she supposed she'd said enough. So she let Len steer her down a corridor and into a room which appeared to be an office of sorts, the driver prudently fading away before they reached the door. Zukie was rather sorry about that, since he seemed almost an ally, or at least more of one than Len.

A man was seated behind the desk. He looked up, not at

Zukie but at Len.

"What were you thinking?" he asked. His voice was calm, but Zukie felt she wouldn't have wanted the question aimed at her.

"She was snooping around."

"So you brought her here."

"Yes, sir."

"It's real hard to get good help, isn't it?" Zukie said sympathetically. "I don't know who you are or what I'm doing here, so why don't we agree it was all a mistake and I'll just leave. Call me a taxi or something if you don't want this goofus involved. I can understand why you wouldn't."

To her astonishment, the man smiled. "You're Mrs Merlino?"

"Yep."

"Mr Romano's cousin."

"Second cousin, but yeah."

"Your reputation has preceded you. Len was wrong to bring you here, but since he did, I will have to make use of you somehow."

"I'm a good cook, if that helps."

"You talk too much," he said. It wasn't a criticism, Zukie decided; he was just stating a fact. "Oh, perhaps I should introduce myself, since we will be spending some time together. I'm Clement Innes."

ZUKIE couldn't honestly say she was too surprised at the announcement, but she didn't think it would be a good idea to let Innes know that she had researched him, or attempted to, anyway.

"OK. And you already know who I am. This is a nice place you got, Clem, but why am I here?"

She heard Len gasp, and guessed that no one had ever addressed Innes that way before. She took a better look at him and saw that her previous idea – that he would be an elderly, pedantic collector – was totally wrong.

Innes couldn't have been more than forty, dark-haired, thin as a rail and dressed casually in jeans and a polo shirt. But he seemed intelligent and had the air of a man born to wealth and privilege. She wondered if he'd become bored with that and decided to dabble in crime as a hobby.

It was hardly a question she could ask at the moment, but she filed it away. At least it didn't appear Innes was going to order Len to take her out and shoot her, so she felt some of her tension easing. And in fact, he looked at Len and said, "Go. Take the van back."

"Yes, sir."

Len wheeled around and went out. Innes watched him go and shook his head just slightly. Then he turned his attention to Zukie.

"You're right; he's not too bright," he said. "Fortunately, he doesn't work for me."

Zukie nodded in complete agreement. "I can see why. Was it him who ripped up the seats in Lou's car? Talk about stupid."

"Yes."

Zukie wasn't sure if he meant Len was stupid or responsible for the car damage, but she felt obliged to keep talking. If nothing else, it would delay the moment when Innes outlined his plans for her immediate future, which she didn't think she really wanted to hear.

"And if that was him and his buddy, they're not very good at burglary, either. But hey, we'll let that go, since they didn't even get the front door open."

Innes sighed, whether at the pair's ineptitude or the fact that Zukie knew they were behind the two acts, she wasn't sure.

"Do you know anything about art, Mrs Merlino?" he asked.

"Not much. Why?"

"How about your cousin?"

"Lou? Probably less than I do. We went to Italy a year or so ago and I had to drag him into the museums. He would have been happy just to sit in a café with a cappuccino."

She knew she was doing Lou a disservice, but she didn't want Innes to think her cousin had any knowledge of whatever scam was going on. All he had done was offer to help a woman jump-start her car, for Pete's sake.

Innes studied her face, which she was attempted to make as innocent as possible. She must have – for once – done a passable job, since he didn't even lift an eyebrow at her comments. Of course, he didn't know her as well as her family and friends did, either.

"I apologize for the attempted burglary and the vandalism," he said finally. "I didn't send them and it wasn't necessary. But you need to understand that I have a problem which needs your cooperation to solve."

Zukie gulped. "What's that?"

"I believe your cousin has something of mine, and I want it back."

THE PARKING enforcement vehicle pulled up behind the illegally parked sedan, and the officer got out to write the ticket. She jotted down the licence plate number and fed it into her tablet. A moment later it popped up with the name and address of the car owner.

Some distant memory of having heard that name before stopped the officer from simply leaving the ticket on the windshield. Instead, she took out her cell phone and made a call.

ON THE other end of the line, Vance was seething, but not at the hapless parking officer. He slammed his phone down.

"Lanigan!"

"Sir?"

"What the hell is your mother-in-law doing leaving her car in a no-parking zone on East Marginal Way?"

Lanigan's jaw dropped. "No idea."

"It's only a block or so from that Minghella Plastics place. She wouldn't have been stupid enough to barge in there and ask if they made fake antiques, would she?"

"I sure hope not. I told her to leave it to us, but you know what's she's like."

"All too well. I don't know how long the car's been there, but five minutes is too long, as far as I'm concerned. See if you can get hold of her, Lanigan. If not, I think we have to assume that she's in some kind of trouble, and much as I would like to leave her there, we're going to have to do something about it."

Chapter 16

Lanigan called the house first, not really expecting that Zukie would be there if her car was a couple of miles away. She wasn't, and neither was Lou.

The next call was to her cell phone, which also drew a blank. Lanigan had no way of knowing this was because Innes had politely invited Zukie to give him her cell phone, and when she reluctantly complied, he had turned it off and locked it in a drawer of the desk.

"Damn," Lanigan muttered, as he got the message that the number was not available.

"Try Romano's cell."

Lanigan called Lou's number. This was more successful, although he had to strain to hear Lou's voice over the sound of crashing bowling pins and background music.

"Lou, it's Jim. Do you happen to know where Zukie is?"

"She said she might go to see Angela. Why?"

Lanigan hesitated, then decided he was going to need all the help he could get, even if it meant upsetting Lou.

"I don't think she went to see Angela. Her car's been found, parked illegally on East Marginal Way. She didn't say anything about going to that plastics factory, did she?"

"Hold on a minute."

Lanigan waited and heard the sound of bowling pins and

music fading into the distance.

"Now what did you say?" Lou asked. "Her car's on East Marginal?"

"That's right. She wasn't in it. The only place anywhere near there we can think of she might have gone was Minghella Plastics, but we don't want to bust in there looking for her unless we're pretty sure that's where she is."

"And even then, I suppose there's no law against it. It's just Zukie being terminally nosy. I told her to mind her own business. You told her to mind her own business. And Vance told her, too. And now look what's happened."

Lou's voice rose in agitation and Lanigan reminded himself that despite their frequent clashes, Lou felt a certain responsibility for his cousin's welfare. And vice versa, of course, which was why she'd gotten involved in the first place.

"Nothing has happened yet, that we know of." Even to Lanigan's own ears, that didn't sound very reassuring. He added, "We'll wait a little longer and see if she comes back to the car. If not, we'll start looking for her."

"Where?"

That was an excellent question and one Lanigan couldn't answer.

"I'll give Angela a call first, just on the chance she went there, and then we'll set things in motion. We'll find her, Lou, don't worry. What's Angela's number?"

AS LANIGAN expected, Angela hadn't seen or heard from her sister that morning.

"She didn't say anything about where she might be going today, did she?"

"No, I haven't talked to her since yesterday and she didn't say anything then."

Lanigan assumed from this that Angela hadn't heard about the abortive burglary, which was a little surprising. He put on his most charming, persuasive voice. "But I bet she's asked you to do some digging for you. I know she says you're really good at finding out things about people."

As he hoped, Angela took this as a compliment.

"Well, yes. I suppose so. It's just that I know people who know people and so on."

"Who did she ask you to find out about? We'll take it for granted that she wanted to know about Shirley Minghella; that was to be expected."

"It sure was. Well, she asked me about somebody called Michael Minghella. I guess he was this Shirley's ex-husband and I think he has something to do with a company called Minghella Plastics. I don't know what the connection is. I suppose his family runs it."

Lanigan appreciated that Angela was only expected to dig up the raw material and turn it over to Zukie for refinement and practical application.

"Zukie didn't say she was going to visit the company, did she?"

"No. Why would she?"

"I don't know. But you probably know better than I do how nosy she can be."

He put a little chuckle into his voice and Angela said, "Boy, do I."

"Was there anything else she asked you about?"

"Hang on, let me think. You know how it is, you get distracted by something or somebody wants you to babysit ..."

Her voice died away and Lanigan had almost decided she was illustrating her point by being distracted from their conversation when she said abruptly, "Innes."

"Pardon?"

"She asked me about somebody called Innes. Clement Innes, that's it. I never heard of him, have you?"

Lanigan unclenched his fingers from the phone.

"Yes, I think I may have. Thanks a million, Angela."

"Wait. Why are you calling *me*, Jim? Doesn't Lou know where she is?"

"No, he doesn't."

"Is Zukie in some kind of trouble?"

"I sincerely hope not."

"Oh, my God. If you're saying that, then she probably is. Jim, you let me know if I can help. I know she's a pain sometimes, but she's still my sister."

"I will, Angela. Thanks again."

He hung up and turned to Vance, who had been listening to his side of the conversation.

"Clement Innes."

"What about him?"

"Zukie was trying to find out about him. She was also trying to find out about Michael Minghella. And we know those two have both been linked to a number of major art robberies and also to each other. It's thought Innes puts in the order, so to speak, and Minghella arranges the actual theft. For a cut of any proceeds, of course, if the item is sold on to another collector. Or payment, if Innes keeps the piece for himself."

Vance nodded in approval. "You've been doing your homework, Lanigan."

"When Zukie is even marginally involved in one of our cases, I find it's a good thing to do. The idea is to stay one step ahead of her. Needless to say, it doesn't always work."

"It hasn't worked this time. Right, we're off to Minghella Plastics. We needed to see them anyway, and now we've got an even better reason. Holt, while we're gone, dig up everything you can find on Clement Innes and Michael Minghella. Come on, Lanigan."

ZUKIE wasn't quite sure what to make of Clement Innes. He was treating her almost as if she was an invited guest in his home, which she clearly wasn't, so she assumed it was because he honestly thought she could lead him to whatever he thought Lou had.

That had to be the *netsuke* that Shirley had planted on him, but the real one, not the fake. Since she didn't have the faintest idea where the real one was, this could present a problem. Zukie swallowed hard and wondered how she would hold up under torture.

In the meantime, Innes had earned a few points by providing her with a cup of coffee, which had been brewed on a fancy machine behind his desk. It was just about the best coffee Zukie had ever tasted, although she had initially been reluctant to accept in case he'd put some kind of drug in it.

Then common sense kicked in. She'd already been knocked out once, she couldn't help him if she was unconscious, and if he tried any truth serum on her – Zukie had read quite a few spy thrillers – it wouldn't matter because she had already told him the truth and had nothing to hide.

So she sipped the coffee and pretended it was just a blip in her normal routine to be kidnapped and transported to the secret lair of a millionaire. If she ever got home, she'd have a fantastic story to tell Shelly and Angela. Jim would scold her for being involved in the first place and Lou probably wouldn't believe a word of it.

"Good coffee," she told Innes.

"Thank you. It's my private blend."

"So I don't suppose I could buy it at the supermarket."

"I'm afraid not."

"That's too bad. You going to tell me what this is all about, Clem? You say it's got something to do with Lou, but honest to God, he doesn't know anything about it and neither do I."

Innes regarded her with something like amusement.

"Oh, we have plenty of time to discuss that, Mrs Merlino."

"Really? Because if I'm not home by dinner time, I can guarantee Lou'll be moving heaven and earth trying to find me. He won't want to go without dinner just because you've got some ridiculous idea he has something of yours. What are we talking about, anyway?"

Innes pushed his chair back and stood up. He was over six feet tall, but Zukie decided not to ask if he had ever played basketball. She suspected he would have been more likely to buy an NBA team franchise out of petty cash.

He had ignored her question, so she added, "Would it hurt to tell me where we are, Clem? I'm guessing Mercer Island or Bellevue."

He ignored that question as well, which made Zukie think she had guessed correctly. She wasn't going to give him the satisfaction of knowing she'd glimpsed water, which narrowed the options, even in the Seattle area. She was also fairly sure they'd negotiated a long, straight stretch of road that was one of the floating bridges crossing the lake to the wealthy suburbs on the far side, but she hadn't dared open her eyes to confirm it.

"Perhaps you'd like a tour."

Zukie suspected he was being sarcastic, so she decided to call his bluff. "Sure, why not?"

To her surprise, he just said, "Come on, then. This way."

Zukie wondered if he was showing her around because he thought she would be awed by her surroundings, because it would make her realize she couldn't get away or because he intended that she wouldn't leave his property alive. She promptly rejected the third option and put a politely interested expression on her face.

Innes guided her down the hallway and into what she identified as a living room, although much larger than any living room she had ever been in. A stone-faced fireplace stretched from floor to ceiling, and two sofas and five armchairs were grouped around it. In Zukie's living room, it had been a stretch to fit in one sofa and two armchairs, and she still bumped into the coffee table occasionally.

On the wall opposite the fireplace, shelves covered the entire wall, filled with an assortment of books, CDs and what Zukie might have classed as travel souvenirs if they hadn't looked like each one cost as much as most people's entire vacations.

Most of them appeared Oriental in origin, made from jade or ivory, and now that Zukie thought about it, the entire room had an Oriental feel to it. Everything was simple, functional and beautifully made.

"Nice room," she said, her eyes scanning the shelves. "You travel a lot?"

"Not that much," Innes said. He followed her gaze. "People bring things to me."

"I guess that would save time, but it wouldn't be nearly as much fun. I haven't travelled very much, but I sure liked our trip to Italy. Course our grandparents came from there, so that made it even more interesting."

"I'm sure it did."

He held out a hand, indicating she should go through the door on the far side of the room. She obeyed, and found herself outside, on a terrace paved with large flat stones. A fire pit sunk into one end was surrounded by built-in benches whose cushions were upholstered in an all-weather fabric. Zukie thought nostalgically of the pair of creaky folding deck chairs in her back yard and hoped she would see them again.

The terrain beyond the terrace was unfamiliar, so she deduced she was now on the opposite side of the house from where Len and his partner had delivered her.

Like the other side, this was landscaped in the Japanese style, with some neatly raked gravel and two more stone lanterns set among the plants. A huge Japanese maple with feathery red leaves stood behind the lanterns.

But what caught Zukie's eye, as she was sure it was meant to do, was a large pond, at least fifteen feet across. As she watched, flashes of brilliant orange, white and black appeared just under the surface, flipped and disappeared again under the dark water. They seemed to sense they had company, because suddenly several of them swam over to where Innes and Zukie were standing, mouths open as if expecting a treat.

"I like your goldfish," she said.

Innes shot her a skeptical look, as if to gauge whether she was being sarcastic. Zukie knew perfectly well the fish were koi carp, but she had decided playing ignorant was her best chance of getting out of the situation in one piece.

"They're koi," Innes said. "I'm sure you must have seen some before."

"Not that size," she said truthfully. "They look like they could take your hand off if you got too close at feeding time."

"They're not carnivorous," he said, "although I admit they will eat a wide variety of food. I give them a carefully balanced diet to keep them healthy. In turn, they give me undemanding companionship."

He spoke almost as if the fish were his children or at least friends, and Zukie decided they were probably a substitute of sorts. If he wasn't intending to use her as a pawn in some kind of illegal operation, she might have felt sorry for him.

"You live here on your own, Clem?" she asked, thinking that she hadn't detected a woman's touch in anything she had seen so far. Or for that matter, much of anybody's touch. The house looked more like a comfortable museum than a home. In that case, she asked herself, why did he need all those sofas and armchairs?

"Except for my staff, yes."

"That's a shame, 'cause I suppose you don't socialize much with your employees. I mean, I haven't seen anyone else here so far except for Len and his buddy and you say they don't work for you. Me, I find it's always nice to have people around to talk to and do things with."

"Which brings us rather neatly to your cousin Lou Romano," Innes said, his eyes still on the fish. "I understand he shares your house."

Zukie nodded. "You should know. That's why those two dropped by to wreck his car and try to break in. What was that about?"

"I didn't send them."

Zukie drew her eyebrows together. "So you keep saying. But you knew about it."

"I know a lot of things, Mrs Merlino."

"Then you ought to know Lou doesn't have the faintest idea what this is all about. And neither do I, Clem."

Innes gave her a probing look. "No? Why were you parked on East Marginal Way?"

Zukie realized she had made a major mistake in trying to have a look at the plastics company, but it was too late to deny she'd been there. Len and his friend had told Innes, and her only hope now was to try to misdirect Innes as to her intentions. She took a deep breath and launched into what she hoped would sound like a reasonable explanation.

"Well, Lou was real upset when Shirley dumped him. You know about Shirley?"

Innes just looked at her. She took that as a sign to proceed.

"So I remembered I'd seen this company called Minghella Plastics and I thought they might be some kind of relation to her and maybe I could find out how to contact her. I didn't tell Lou what I was doing, which I suppose I should have, but you know what men are like, always trying to tell women not to do things."

"Which does not appear to work in your case."

"Jeez, you're as bad as Lou. Anyway, I went down there, but before I could talk to anybody, those two gorillas grabbed me and brought me here. And so here I am."

"Yes, here you are, Mrs Merlino. Are you trying to tell me that Mr Romano harbored some sort of notion of reconnecting with Ms Minghella?"

"I don't know, do I? Lou didn't tell me. He just sulked a lot."

Innes was standing about two feet from Zukie. With no warning whatsoever, his hand shot out and closed over her wrist, so tightly that she yelped with pain. She tried to yank it free, and he let go, but not before she felt like the wrist bones had been ground together. She rubbed it and glared at him.

"What the heck was that for?"

"I don't like incompetence and I don't like liars," Innes said. "You and Mr Romano both know perfectly well that there is no chance of a resumption of their relationship because Ms Minghella is dead. Would you like to start again and tell me what you were really doing snooping around that factory?"

Chapter 17

For a moment, Zukie just glared at him. She tried to collect her thoughts, chief among them being the fact that this guy was smarter than she had first thought and she could be in real danger. She rubbed her wrist again.

"That wasn't necessary, you know," she said.

"Perhaps not. But I think now we understand each other, don't we?"

"Yeah. I understand that you're trying to bully me into telling you about something I don't know anything about. I couldn't tell you anything even if I wanted to. So you're basically wasting your time, and mine, too."

She braced her feet, expecting him to react violently and ready to fight back. But he just gazed at her, and she met his eyes defiantly.

"You really don't know, do you?" he said slowly.

Zukie shrugged. "Without knowing what you're talking about, I can't say, but my guess would be no."

"So what were you doing by Minghella Plastics?"

Zukie held up her hands. "This is the truth, Clem, so help me. Lou had a few dates with Shirley Minghella. Then they were out at the mall and there was a little … incident … and he thought she had set him up so somebody almost ran over him. No idea why. Kind of put the kibosh on his feelings for her, so he decided not to see her again. Next thing we know, there was a homicide detective on the doorstep telling us she was dead.

"Now if something like that had happened to your cousin, you'd be curious, too. Being as her name was the same as that factory and being as the cops wouldn't tell us anything, I decided to drop by and see if anybody there knew anything. Could be it's a different Minghella family altogether. But I didn't even get through the door before Len and his buddy grabbed me, so if there's some deep, dark secret there, it's still there."

She stood and waited, thinking she had done a good job of presenting her case. Everything she had told Innes this time was true; it was just that she had left out large chunks of information. The whole *netsuke* saga, for example; the postcard Shirley had sent to Lou and how Shirley had picked him up in the first place.

She hadn't mentioned the wrecked car seats or the burglary attempt, either, but it seemed he was already aware of those, whether or not he was behind them. So she was satisfied that she'd come clean, or relatively clean, and hoped Innes would believe that was all she knew. From his earlier remark, she gathered that he didn't think too highly of her intelligence and she was happy to leave it that way.

"Come with me," he said abruptly, and turned back to the house. Zukie followed reluctantly, resisting a momentary impulse to turn and take off through the landscaped grounds. She knew she wouldn't get far and she was also curious to know what exactly Innes planned to do with her.

Common sense told her that if he had planned to kill her, he would have already done it. From what he'd said, he had in mind using her as some sort of bargaining chip, which gave her more scope. Zukie was realistic about her talents in life, but she had great faith in her ability to talk her way out of just about any situation.

So she followed Innes back into the house without comment. He indicated the chairs by the fireplace and said, "Wait there."

"OK."

She sank into butter-soft leather and settled herself

comfortably. Innes went on through to his office and she could hear his voice speaking to someone, but not the actual words. Creeping closer to eavesdrop wasn't really an option, so she stayed put, her eyes roaming over the collection of art objects on the shelves.

Two things happened simultaneously. She heard Innes say, "No. I'm sure of it," and she saw something on the shelf that looked very familiar, an object she hadn't noticed before.

She didn't dare go over and take a closer look, for fear he would come back into the room, but she was positive that the small ivory fish on the shelf, nestled between two other *netsuke*, was a twin of the one Lou had handed over to the police.

So if the real *netsuke* was here – and she couldn't see Innes displaying a replica – why did he think Lou had it? Or perhaps he already knew Lou had had the replica and for some reason, he wanted it back.

VANCE angled the unmarked police car into a space not far from Zukie's. In his case, it was a legal parking space, but that was the least of his concerns. He and Lanigan got out and walked over to her car, circling it but not touching anything.

The car seemed undamaged, Lanigan was pleased to see; no dents, bloodstains, ripped seats or any signs at all of a struggle. It was locked, but then Zukie always locked her car when she wasn't in it, even for a minute.

The parking ticket was stuck under a windshield wiper, but they left that, too.

"She can pay it herself," Vance said. "Serves her right for the amount of trouble she causes."

Lanigan was glad Vance was using present tense in referring to his mother-in-law, even though he agreed with the sentiment.

"OK, let's have a quick look at Minghella Plastics," Vance said. "And no suggestion that they're anything but a genuine, law-abiding company, which for all we know, they may be."

"Right."

They walked up to the front door and Vance pushed it open. A young woman behind a reception desk looked at them curiously.

"Hello, can I help you?"

"I don't know yet," Vance said pleasantly. He displayed his identification and Lanigan followed suit. "Detective Lee Vance, Seattle Police. We're looking for a missing person."

"A missing person?" The girl furrowed her forehead. "Why would we know anything about a missing person?"

"Because her car was found parked on the street just up from you. We'll be asking all the businesses along here, so don't think you've been singled out."

Neither officer missed the relief that flickered across the receptionist's face for a second.

"Who is it who's missing?"

"A woman in her fifties. Lanigan, do you have the description?"

Lanigan pretended to consult his notepad. "Caucasian female, fifty-nine years old, five-foot-four, 145 pounds, black hair with some gray, brown eyes."

He cast his mind back to Zukie's usual apparel and added, "Last seen wearing jeans, sweatshirt, track shoes and a black parka."

"She might have seemed a little confused," Vance said. "Maybe you could ask if anyone's seen her wandering around here? She might have come into the building not realizing what it was."

"I've been on the reception desk all morning and no one like that's come in," the receptionist said. As neither Vance nor Lanigan showed signs of leaving, she said, "All right, I'll ask."

"Thank you. The family is very worried."

That was certainly true, Lanigan thought. It had taken a great deal of persuasion to stop Lou from insisting that he come along with them, once he had decided that she was in danger, and Lanigan himself was more concerned than he had let on. Annoying as Zukie could be at times, he liked her immensely and didn't want her to come to any harm.

The receptionist picked up her phone and spoke to someone, relaying the description she'd been given. The officers could hear the response even before she told them – no, no one had seen a woman like that around the building.

"All right, thank you," Vance said. He handed her a business card. "Obviously, if anyone remembers anything or sees her, please let us know."

"Sure."

Vance and Lanigan went back outside and exchanged glances.

"She was here," Vance said, and Lanigan nodded. "The question is: Did she go or was taken somewhere else, or is she still on site?"

"I wonder if Michael Minghella is around," Lanigan said. "He's the most likely one to have had contact with her, don't you think?"

"What I think is that we're going to have to get some backup. The two of us can't raid the building without probable cause, and I don't think a parked car qualifies, however sure we are that she's here. Or at least that she *was* here. Call the art robbery guys. They've been watching Minghella, so see if they know where he is."

Lanigan took out his cell phone as they walked back to the police car. He started to make the call, but Vance suddenly said, "Wait a second."

Across the street and a block north of Minghella Plastics was a trash can, and rooting through it was an elderly man dressed in a motley collection of clothes. He pulled a bottle from the trash and held it up, perusing it thoughtfully before putting it carefully back in the receptacle.

"Think he might have seen something?" Lanigan asked.

"Pink elephants, most likely. But it won't hurt to ask."

They crossed the street and approached the man, who looked up in alarm.

"Good afternoon," Vance said. "We're police officers; do you have a minute to answer a couple of questions for us?"

"Cops?"

"Nothing to worry about," Lanigan assured him, trying not to recoil visibly from the aroma of sweat and stale beer. "We just want to know if you might have seen a particular person around this area today."

"Who?" The man looked poised for flight.

Vance repeated Zukie's description and said, "She isn't in any trouble and neither will you be. We just want to find her. Have you seen her?"

The man appeared to be consulting his memory. Finally he said, "She gave me a buck. Sounds like her, anyway, except she had kind of reddish hair."

"A wig," Lanigan said to Vance. "It's her favorite one."

The man was still thinking. "You could maybe ask those other two guys."

Lanigan swallowed. "What other two guys would that be?"

"The ones she got into a fight with. Over there." He gestured at Minghella Plastics.

"OK, let's back up a minute," Vance said calmly. "The woman gave you a dollar. Then what happened?"

"She walked past that building. Two guys came out from the back and grabbed her. She kicked and punched but they dragged her round the back. Then right after that, a van drove out and took off real fast."

"Going which way?" Lanigan asked.

The man flung out a grimy hand, pointing.

"North," Vance said. "Can you remember any details at all about the van? Size, color, any writing on it?"

This question brought another lengthy mental consultation. "Big white van with some letters on the side. Two letters, MP, in a circle."

"Excellent," Vance said. "Any other details at all?"

The man shook his head regretfully.

"How about the two men? Any description you can give us?"

"I was too far away to see much. Big guys, and mean. Sorry; that's all."

"That's all right. You've been extremely helpful. Thank you, sir."

They left him in contemplation of his trash can and went back to the police car.

"Traffic cams, Holt," Vance said into his phone. "East Marginal Way, between Michigan and Lucille, any time from about nine this morning onward. White van, letters MP, that's Mike Papa, in a circle on the side, two men in it."

"I'm on it. Sounds like you've got something."

"Maybe. See what you can dig up. Did they get any hits on the two who tried to get into Mrs Merlino's house?"

A pause and then Holt said, "Tentatively identified as Leonard McCann and Robert Travis. Small-time crooks. Both apparently employed by Minghella Plastics, and therefore with a link to Michael Minghella."

"Which means they could be the pair who were in the van. We need to find them and the van, not necessarily in that order."

"Yes, sir."

Vance closed the phone. Lanigan said, "It sounds like they took Zukie."

"Yes, it does," Vance said, "if he saw her fighting with them and then the van taking off. They're probably regretting that now."

Lanigan couldn't argue the point.

"But why would they snatch her?" he asked. "She doesn't have any information and isn't a threat to them. And there's no point at all in trying to swap her for someone else or getting a ransom paid."

"Hell, no. If she's anything like she normally is, they'd pay to get rid of her."

Lanigan couldn't argue with that, either.

"How does Clement Innes fit into this, do you think?"

"Well, let's see," Vance said. "Innes is filthy rich. He collects fine art, especially Asian antiquities. He's known for being a recluse, hardly ever leaving his property. I've got Holt digging to see what else she can find, but we already know he's been tied to Minghella, who's been tied to various art thefts. It looks like there's a kind of chain that the stolen objects pass along, which reduces the chance of any one person getting caught with the goods. My guess is that Lou Romano accidentally interrupted that chain."

"Or Shirley Minghella used him to interrupt it."

"Yes, that's entirely possible, too. It looks like she planted something on him which turned out to be a fake. The question is: Did she know it was a fake?"

Lanigan frowned. "Regardless of whether she knew, Zukie knows it was a fake, and that it could well have been made at Minghella Plastics. Do you think it was Innes who ordered her snatched?"

"Maybe. Or Michael Minghella, although I'm inclined to think not, because he already had her on site here. If the van took off with her in it, it would have been more likely to be going to Innes."

"If so, that's going to be tricky, being as we can't just invade his property looking for a possible kidnap victim without any proof she's there."

"That's right. So we'll see what the traffic cams show and if that van can be traced anywhere near Innes's property, we'll have our probable cause. We'll find her, Lanigan, assuming she doesn't drive Innes nuts in the meantime."

Lanigan visualized Zukie telling an art-collecting millionaire who had kidnapped her what she thought of him. As it happened, it was a remarkably accurate picture.

"Shall I tell Lou what we think happened?"

"Not yet. Tell him we have a couple of good leads, but no details. The last thing I want is him chasing off to rescue her or insisting he comes along with us. Call him on the way back to the precinct."

INNES CAME out of his office and surveyed Zukie, who gave him a bright smile.

"Can I go now?" she asked.

"Not yet."

That sounded encouraging, as if she would be released sometime, so Zukie decided not to pursue the point.

"Any chance of some lunch, Clem?" she asked "That stuff Len used made me feel kind of sick at first, but I'm better now and it's been a while since I had breakfast. Being as you have such good coffee, I reckon you've got good food here, too."

Innes glanced at a wristwatch that had probably cost more than Zukie's car.

"All right. Come on."

Zukie struggled up out of the comfortable chair and followed him down the hall and into a room she hadn't seen yet. It was obviously a kitchen, but outfitted with an array of cupboards and appliances that made her eyes widen.

"Wow. This is really something."

She thought he thawed a little at the response, and wondered if he did his own cooking or hired a team of chefs. He could easily have fit several of them into the kitchen, she felt sure. But the room was currently empty of human life, and he went to a silver-doored appliance that she tentatively identified as a refrigerator.

"Do you like sushi?"

"Not that much," Zukie said truthfully. "Heck, a peanut butter sandwich would be fine."

Innes shot her a glance as if to judge whether she was joking.

"No peanut butter, but I do have almond butter."

"Sounds good. Do you do your own cooking?"

"Sometimes. I employ a chef but usually only for evening meals."

"If I had a kitchen like this, you'd never get me out of it. I love to cook, especially when I'm stressed about something. It's cheaper than therapy and you get to eat the results."

Innes almost smiled at that, she was sure. He took a loaf of bread and a jar from one of the cupboards, and a table knife from a concealed drawer. Zukie watched as he spread something resembling peanut butter on the bread and then added a layer of what she thought must be jam of some kind. He cut the finished sandwich in half and put it on a plate, sliding it across a wide marble counter. Zukie hoisted herself onto a padded stool and took the plate.

"I hope that meets your high standards, Mrs Merlino."

"Thanks. Aren't you eating anything?"

"Not at the moment."

Zukie shook her head. "Don't skip meals, Clem. It's not good for you and you could stand to put on a few pounds. You're way too thin."

She took a bite of her sandwich. The almond butter had a slightly different taste, but the jam was apricot and almost as good as the kind she made every year from the bags of apricots Angela brought her from eastern Washington. The bread was delicious, too, possibly one of those artisan breads that Colonna's deli kept on hand for its more upmarket customers.

Before she could stop herself, Zukie said, "You ever buy anything at Colonna's, Clem? It's a real good deli and bakery on Beacon Hill."

"No," he said sharply.

"OK, it was just a question. This is good bread like theirs, that's all."

Zukie was tempted to ask him if he knew Shirley had been there with Lou, but decided against it. The less contact he thought she had with Shirley the better, and after all, she had only met the woman once for a few minutes. She finished off the sandwich and Innes poured her another cup of coffee, then one for himself.

"And now, Mrs Merlino," he said, sitting down opposite her, "we have to decide what to do with you."

Chapter 18

Holt had been busy, and by the time Vance and Lanigan returned to the precinct, she had accumulated a file of information on the various players.

"Good work," Vance said, once his team was assembled. "Let's go over this and put everything in some kind of order. Then we'll decide the best way to proceed. Stop chewing your nails, Lanigan. The last thing we want is to charge in there and spook Innes. We'll get her out."

"If she's there."

"Oh, I think she is. Go on, Holt."

"Right." Holt cleared her throat. "Traffic cams show a van matching that description going north on East Marginal at 10:13 a.m. It picked up I-90 at Dearborn a few minutes later and went east across the bridge to Mercer Island. It exited I-90 on Island Crest Way, going south."

"Well, that's a break," Vance said. "That will save us the trouble of searching the entire east side and by extension, the rest of the country. And Clement Innes lives on Mercer Island. Owns a chunk of it, a lakefront estate. What a coincidence. Where did the van go after it left I-90, do we know?"

"They don't have cameras the whole length of the island, but as far as we can tell, it went toward the southeast corner of the island."

Vance nodded. "That's where his estate is."

"And then it was seen coming back north – making the trip in reverse – not long afterwards. The van returned to East Marginal Way at 11:18."

"Good. I don't suppose we can get them for speeding, or using a cell phone while driving, or anything useful like that?"

"Sorry, no."

"I hate law-abiding criminals. Has the van gone anywhere else since then?"

"Not that we could see."

Vance turned to Lanigan. "Do we have Mrs Merlino's prints and DNA on file?"

"Yes."

"So we can learn if she was in the van." Lanigan started to say something and Vance said, "Yes, I know, the first thing is to find her and get her out safely. The DNA will be useful later. Holt, do you have the van plate?"

"Yes, sir."

"Check with Olympia and see who it's registered to."

"Already done. Minghella Plastics."

"Good. Give me everything you have about the connection between Michael Minghella and Clement Innes. I know some of it, but the rest of the team may not."

"Right." Holt looked through her papers and selected one. "Michael Minghella, fifty-five, appears to be the black sheep of his family, who have run a perfectly respectable Georgetown factory making small molded plastic objects for the past forty years. His brother Steven is the current boss there. No criminal record for him.

"Michael, on the other hand, started working at the family firm but seems to have decided it was too dull and boring. About fifteen years ago, he was suspected to have been behind a theft of ivory artifacts – Alaskan ivory carvings. They had been on display in a gallery and when the owner went to take them back, he discovered the original ivory had been replaced by very clever hard plastic imitations. Evidence pointed to Minghella having made the substitution, but the case fell apart in court and he was never convicted."

"What evidence are we talking about?" Vance asked.

"Security camera footage showing him in the gallery at the relevant time and testimony from the gallery owner as to Minghella asking a lot of questions and actually handling some of the carvings."

"So we assume he learned from that experience to be more discreet."

"Apparently. Over the years, there have been several similar incidents – substitutions and thefts – but Minghella has managed to avoid being ID'd. On the other hand, McCann and Travis have been seen in the vicinity, but again, no concrete evidence. You can see why the art robbery detail are getting fed up about not getting a conviction, since some of these collections are worth hundreds of thousands of dollars."

"And where does Shirley Minghella come into the picture?"

Holt turned to another page.

"Michael Minghella and Shirley Carson were married not long before his arrest over the ivory theft. There's no indication that she was involved or even knew about it."

"A short marriage, then, if they were divorced about ten years ago."

"Yes, less than five years. We could speculate that she found out what Michael was doing and ditched him. Or there may have been another reason; we don't know. At any rate, after that, Shirley went off to travel the world and Michael was left behind in every sense."

"Traveling the world isn't the cheap option," Vance said. "Are you sure she didn't benefit from the theft? Items being sold on, for example?"

"No. She comes from a wealthy family and bank records show that she had her own money well before marrying Minghella."

"OK, fair enough. Has she been back to Seattle since then? Before this most recent time?"

"Yes, but if you're thinking her return trips were timed to coincide with her ex's activities, I'm afraid not. Not until this last one."

The room was silent for a moment. Finally Vance said, "OK, what's the theory on the Innes collection? He loaned it to the art museum, right?"

"Yes, that's right. But here's the interesting part. His collection was the largest part of the exhibit, but there was another exhibitor involved as well. A man called Sawyer, Edward Sawyer."

"Let me guess," Lanigan said. "Innes got his stuff back OK but Mr Sawyer didn't."

ZUKIE WAS getting a little tired of captivity, even a luxurious captivity such as this one. Aside from a sore wrist, she couldn't say she'd been mistreated, but it was irritating not to know what was going on, or whether anyone had even noticed yet that she was missing.

And if they had noticed – for example, if Lou had come back to the house or tried to call her cell phone – how on earth would they work out where she might be? Besides which, she belatedly remembered she had parked her car illegally and probably it had a ticket on it by now or had been towed away.

She wished now she had followed Lou and Lanigan's advice and kept her nose out of the investigation, but it was too late to worry about that. The main issue at this point was to get out of Innes's clutches in one piece and just possibly, discover what, if anything, he had to do with Shirley's death.

Innes was watching her with the same concentration as a cat watching a bird, and she felt uneasy, as if he were reading her mind. She hated it when people did that.

"So what do you do all day?" she asked him. "You obviously got lots of money; did you inherit it or do you run some kind of business?"

"A little of both. I buy and sell things."

"Don't suppose you're going to tell me what kind of things."

He raised his eyebrows. "I thought you had already worked that out."

"Clem, I don't know diddly about your business, and what's more, I don't really care. I was just trying to be friendly."

"You amaze me, Mrs Merlino," he said, a ghost of a smile crossing his face. "I could have you shot and dump your body in the lake, and no one would ever know what happened to you, let alone connect me with it. But here you are, making wisecracks. I'm beginning to think you really don't know what you've landed yourself in."

"I didn't land myself in anything, Clem. Those two idiots grabbed me off the street, remember?"

"Yes." The tone of Innes's voice made Zukie glad she wasn't one of the idiots.

"So there's no point in keeping me here."

She hoped that didn't sound like a suggestion that she should be shot and dumped in the lake, but at least Innes's comment had confirmed that she was on a lakefront estate. Not that it would help much if no one knew she was there.

"I'm beginning to agree with that. How does Mr Romano put up with you?"

"Lou's my second cousin. He's stuck with me. You can choose your friends, but not your family. And you can choose to be sensible and let me go."

Innes shook his head. "Unbelievable. Come on. It's time to feed the koi."

He opened the fridge and took out a carton. Zukie hopped down from the stool and followed him outside again, crossing the terrace to the fish pond. The koi obviously knew it was time for their food, since they promptly swam over to the side, forming a seething mass of orange, white and black bodies, mouths upturned.

Zukie glanced at Innes, who was smiling at them.

"Guess they're kind of a substitute for friends, huh?"

"They're more intelligent than most friends would be."

"If you're talking about Len and his buddy, I couldn't agree more."

Innes opened the carton and took out some fresh lettuce leaves and orange slices, tossing them to the fish and watching them attack the food. When the lettuce and oranges were gone, he opened a small box attached to the side of the tank and took out a scoopful of pellets, scattering them over the pond. The koi churned the water as they went after the pellets, knocking each other out of the way and clamoring for more.

"Jeez, they're really hungry," Zukie said. "What happens if they get fed the wrong stuff?"

"Someone gets into trouble," Innes said. "Don't even think it."

"I wasn't. They're real pretty fish."

"Yes, they are." Innes closed the box and gave the koi a last fond look.

"My sister used to have a goldfish pond but a heron ate her fish," Zukie told him. "You ever have a hungry heron or cormorant or something get into your pond? I know they're big fish, but still."

"No. Nothing and no one is allowed near the fish pond without my permission."

That seemed to be the end of that discussion, although Zukie wondered just how he discouraged large birds or even racoons who might see his pets as lunch. She wasn't sure she wanted to know. Innes had been reasonably polite to her, but she thought he was just a little crazy.

VANCE and his crew had come to much the same conclusion, but with less first-hand evidence.

"Let's hear what happened with the *netsuke*," he suggested.

"I can only give you a few hard facts," Holt said. "The rest would be guesswork and trying to connect the dots."

"Give us the facts and then we'll look at the dots."

"Right. Clement Innes collects all kinds of artifacts, but

especially Japanese and Chinese ones. He's especially fond of small jade and ivory objects – small carvings, snuffboxes, *netsuke*. And like all collectors who are passionate about something, there's always going to be the one piece they would love to have but can't get their hands on. Either it costs too much or it's so rare that it's simply not available."

"Or someone else owns it and won't let go," Vance said.

"Exactly. Now Innes has his collection, and it's pretty impressive. He buys pieces at auction, and he also has agents in Asia who keep their eyes open and buy pieces for him there. Nothing illegal or immoral about any of that."

"OK."

"Until he got to the point, about five years ago, when he couldn't get his hands on some rare ivory *netsuke*. He wanted it in the worst way, but the guy who owned it refused to sell, even when Innes offered him over the going price. This is all from the art theft guys, by the way. There was talk going round about how desperate he was.

"So having failed to buy it legitimately, he apparently decided to steal it. Or to be precise, to have Michael Minghella, or someone working with him, steal it. Minghella had started up a racket, getting the basic material from his brother's factory, which he was then selling as ivory when in fact it was plastic.

"Excellent imitations, just to look at, but of course they wouldn't stand up to close examination. He had been implicated in several thefts where objects had been on display in a gallery and then when the exhibitor got them back, they weren't the originals, like the Alaskan ivory I mentioned earlier."

"I trust Innes wasn't ever one of his victims."

"No, but word gets around and it seems Innes decided to make use of Minghella and his talents. So when the *netsuke*'s legitimate owner loaned his collection to a gallery, Minghella was waiting in the wings with an excellent copy. He's a very talented artist, by the way. It's just unfortunate that he's also a greedy criminal."

Lanigan raised a hand.

"Is this the fish *netsuke* we're talking about?"

"Not yet. That comes later."

"All right," Vance said. "So Innes and Minghella hooked up and Minghella stole the *netsuke* for him. Successfully, we assume, because it was the first of several similar substitutions. Now let's move to the current case. How does Shirley Minghella fit into it?"

"Well, this is where we leave the facts and turn to a certain amount of guesswork. Shirley had been in Japan for a while and she had become quite knowledgeable about Japanese art and antiques. When she returned to Seattle, Michael contacted her, apparently thinking enough time had gone by since the divorce that she wouldn't mind helping him with a little project. Actually a fairly large project, since we aren't talking about a small gallery this time, but a major art museum with serious security."

"Ah," Lanigan said. "And she said, sure, she'd be glad to help out, but instead she went to SPD. So he must have told her what he was planning to do."

"It seems so. The art guys checked her out, found no criminal record, decided she was genuine about helping them take down Minghella, and signed her up."

"That was an extremely dangerous game she was playing," said Detective Graham, who was in the chair next to Lanigan. "If there's one thing we know about both Minghella and Innes, it's that they don't stand for treachery in the ranks."

Silence descended as they all reflected that Graham was absolutely correct, and that Shirley had paid the ultimate price for her double allegiance.

"So Minghella recruited Shirley to act as an adviser, an expert on Japanese art, which she could do convincingly thanks to her stay there. She was to pretend to be Innes's associate, supervising the display of his artifacts. In that role, she would have the opportunity to do the switch, swapping the fakes for the real *netsuke*. Or at least the ones that Innes wanted to add to his collection, such as the fish. We know this much, because she kept SPD informed on what Minghella had planned."

"And then everything fell apart," Vance said. "Right, I think we can make a guess as to what happened, even if we don't know exactly why she roped Lou Romano in. We may never know the whole story. However, his involvement has created a real problem, in that someone – probably Innes – thinks Romano knows more than he does, and probably thinks Shirley passed one of the genuine *netsuke* on to him rather than giving it to Minghella to pass on to Innes. But she didn't. The one she planted on him was a fake."

"So what the …" Lanigan stopped. "So where's the real fish? If I'm following this, the fish belonged to someone else, but Innes wanted it stolen for himself."

"That's right. We don't know where the real one went, but Romano doesn't have it."

"My theory, for what it's worth," Vance said, "is that given the mess caused by this latest theft, and Romano's involvement, Innes has now decided Minghella is a liability rather than an asset. So he's going to accuse him of stealing something – maybe that ivory fish, which is worth thousands on its own – and make sure he gets nailed for it, while keeping his own reputation squeaky clean. Or he might just skip the fake charge and hire those two men to take out Minghella, as quickly and quietly as possible. We know they're capable of it, because we've already got some evidence linking them to Shirley's murder."

There were solemn nods around the room.

"Leonard McCann and Robert Travis," Holt said. "DNA found in her condo matches theirs, but a good defence lawyer might be able to explain that away. And on a less serious charge, they also ripped up Romano's car and attempted to break into his house. Fingerprints on the car; security cam footage on the attempted B and E."

"Mrs Merlino's house," Vance corrected her. "Just about the dumbest thing they could have done, since that made her mad enough to go after them, and by extension, Michael Minghella.

Her car was abandoned near the plastics factory, and a witness saw her fighting with two men, after which a van took off for Mercer Island. It doesn't take too much imagination to work out that's where she is."

"Why does Innes want her?" Graham asked. "She isn't involved."

"I have a feeling he *didn't* want her," Vance said. "McCann and Travis are not terribly intelligent and they're also a little too impulsive. It's even possible that they were acting on their own initiative and not anyone's orders when they shot Shirley, assuming they were responsible. They're Minghella's men, after all, not Innes's, but I'm willing to bet they're available to the highest bidder. Regardless, if Mrs Merlino is with Innes and she hasn't driven him stark raving mad yet, we have to get her out. Carefully. I'm open to suggestions."

INNES was on the phone again, leaving Zukie in the luxurious living room with orders not to leave it. He had accompanied this with something resembling a smile, but for once, Zukie had no intention of disobeying. She had decided her best chance of survival depended on not antagonizing Innes too much, so she was trying to be agreeable.

However, she couldn't help but wonder when someone would notice she wasn't around and raise the alarm. Or perhaps they already knew and were sneaking through the wooded estate, on their way to rescue her.

If she was outside, would that be better, making her easier to find? Or was she safer in the house, in case there was a gun battle? She hated to think of the lovely leather furniture being riddled by bullets, but at least she could hide behind it.

Her thoughts were interrupted by Innes returning.

"Who's likely to notice you're gone?" he asked abruptly.

"All kinds of people," Zukie said innocently. "Lou, of course; my sister, 'cause I usually phone her every afternoon; my daughter, my son-in-law, my neighbors, the people at Colonna's

… see what you're missing by living out here by yourself?"

"I'm not missing anything."

"Oh, and I left my car in a no-parking zone, so that means I've probably got a ticket by now. I hope you're going to pay it for me."

Innes frowned at her. "That was stupid."

"Well, I was only planning to be there a few minutes. And it's not my fault I couldn't move it."

"So the police department knows your car's been abandoned."

The thought cheered Zukie, but she didn't want to share that.

"The parking enforcement guys, that's all."

"Let's hope that's all. In the meantime, I'm expecting a visitor."

"That's nice."

"It's not a social visit. He's a … business associate."

"OK. I'll stay out of it, if you boys need to talk business. I'll go talk to the fish or something."

"Oh, no, Mrs Merlino," Innes said. "I want you in on the discussion. My associate's name is Michael Minghella."

Chapter 19

Vance outlined his plan to remove Zukie from Innes's custody, a simple but effective procedure which involved the participation of the Mercer Island police. This was on the theory that not only was it was their patch, but they would also be more familiar with the terrain and Innes himself.

"Smart, rich and unstable," had been their assessment, and after hearing Holt's report, no one in Vance's team would disagree. "Let's hope he hasn't fed your lady to the koi carp."

"They're not piranhas," Vance had said. "Let's keep a sense of perspective. OK, here's what we'll do."

ZUKIE HAD no great desire to meet Michael Minghella, even though she admitted having a certain amount of curiosity. To her knowledge, she had never before met a hardened career criminal – which she assumed he was – and wondered if you could tell by looking at them how dishonest they were.

On the other hand, she had once initially failed to identify someone she knew fairly well as a murderer, and in another case, someone she was actually related to. So it would be interesting, and if she managed to come out of the meeting unscathed, she might even have a wealth of useful information to pass on to the police.

Zukie was also a little unsettled to realize that she had

misjudged Innes as well. She had been thinking he was an innocent victim – someone whose cherished possessions had been substituted and stolen by Minghella and his associates – and it was something of a shock to learn he was up to his ears in the scam. After all, if he wasn't, why would he call Minghella a business associate?

Since there wasn't much else she could do, she settled down in one of the leather chairs to wait. When Innes went into the kitchen for a few minutes, she darted another look at the *netsuke* on his shelf. It was very much like the one Lou had been given and which had been handed over to the police, but she wouldn't swear it was identical. However, from her vantage point across the room, she thought Innes's fish looked a little darker and more worn, as it should if it was made of hundred-year-old ivory rather than modern plastic.

Zukie dragged her attention away from the little fish as Innes came back into the room.

"He'll be here shortly," he told her. "Your part is to listen and answer honestly anything you're asked. Is that clear?"

Zukie resented being treated like a naughty child, although she knew talking back – her favorite tactic when she had *been* a naughty child – wasn't the wisest course of action. So she just said, "Sure thing, Clem."

"And don't call me that."

"OK, Mr Innes."

A buzzer sounded and Innes went to an intercom on the wall.

"Yes?"

"Mr Minghella is here."

"Send him through."

The intercom clicked off and Innes fixed her with what he probably thought was a cold stare. Having dealt with a succession of stern nuns, three older brothers and Lou, Zukie was unmoved.

"Remember what I said," he said.

"Yep."

Another buzzer sounded and Innes went out of the room. He

returned a moment later accompanied by a smartly dressed man in his fifties, with dark hair graying at the temples and sharp brown eyes. They rested on Zukie, who smiled politely.

"Michael Minghella, Susanna Merlino," Innes said. "At least I assume you two haven't met before."

"No, we haven't," Minghella said, smiling back at her.

"Don't think so," Zukie said, trying to remember if she'd ever seen him at the Plane View restaurant. He seemed vaguely familiar and with the family company located in the same general area, it was always possible. He didn't exactly look like a criminal, either. And with his Italian good looks and his confident personality, she could see why Shirley had been attracted to him, even if she'd had the good sense to dump him later.

"I'm sure I would have remembered," she added.

Innes gave her a look which was intended to squelch her completely.

"Have a seat, Michael," he said. "Coffee?"

Zukie gave Innes a look of approval. He might be a criminal of sorts, and of course he wasn't Italian, but at least he understood the rudiments of hospitality.

"I'd have some if I were you," she told Minghella. "It's real good coffee."

"No, thank you," Minghella said.

"I wouldn't mind a cup," Zukie said.

Innes ignored her. "Michael, we have things to discuss. Ordinarily, I would keep this a private conversation, but unfortunately, Mrs Merlino has become involved in our … transaction."

Minghella nodded. "I know. Very unfortunate."

"So what should have been a smooth operation has become a total shambles. We can't, however, blame this totally on Mrs Merlino."

"No."

"Damn right you can't," Zukie said.

Innes gave her another look.

"Sorry, but it's true."

"Be quiet." Innes turned back to Minghella. "We've been working together a long time, Michael, but I think the time has come to terminate the relationship."

Zukie gulped and hoped he wouldn't shoot Minghella on the spot. Aside from anything else, it would wreck the pristine living room.

"But first, perhaps you could explain to me exactly what your former wife's role was in turning this operation inside out. I know she went to the cops and ratted you out; that much is obvious. That alone means I would never trust you again, even assuming you somehow managed to stay out of jail. But why did she drag this Romano character into it?"

That was precisely the question Zukie most wanted answered – along with whether she would leave Innes's estate alive – so she pricked her ears up.

"He wasn't meant to be involved at all," Minghella said. "Hell, if Shirley wanted to screw the guy, it's nothing to do with me. We've been divorced a long time, and I didn't care one way or the other. Her role in this operation – it was strictly business."

"So what happened?" Innes asked.

Minghella spread his hands out in a gesture of incomprehension.

"Honest to God, I don't know. I mean, I know what happened, but not why."

"Try me. Start at the beginning."

"OK. You got your stuff first, as per the agreement."

"Yes." Innes's eyes flicked to the shelf where the fish *netsuke* was, then back, so quickly that if Zukie hadn't been watching, she would have missed it. She deduced that it was a good thing for Minghella that he'd at least honored that part of the deal.

"I'd given Shirley the replica to put in the exhibit when it ended, so you'd get the real one and Sawyer would end up with the replica. She promised she would and I had no reason to doubt her. But instead of putting it where it should have gone, with his stuff, she pocketed the damn thing. Said she'd give it back to me if I stopped the racket. That's what she called it, a racket."

Minghella sounded indignant and Zukie almost commented, but stopped herself in time.

"Was that Romano's influence?" Innes asked.

"Don't be stupid," Zukie said, forgetting her promise to be quiet. "Lou didn't have any idea what you guys were up to. He just thought Shirley was a nice person to spend some time with. If he'd known she was mixed up in something like this, he'd have run a mile."

She stopped because they were both staring at her. For the first time, it dawned on her that Shirley's dead car battery might actually have been genuine and not a ruse to involve Lou in some criminal scheme. That made at least two people she'd been wrong about, which was embarrassing. She reckoned she must be losing her touch.

"So you see I was really stuck between a rock and a hard place," Minghella said, as if she hadn't spoken. "If she kept it, it would have been obvious that something was missing from the collection. If she gave it back to me, I'd have to work out a way to put it into Sawyer's collection without alerting him something was off. A real problem, either way."

"So you decided that shooting your ex-wife was the sensible solution to this problem?" Innes's voice dripped sarcasm.

"I didn't do that, Clement. Yeah, I was pissed off at her, but not to that extent."

Innes didn't respond, and Minghella continued his narrative.

"I set up a meet with her, out at the mall. I was there way ahead of time, to check it out, and who do I see but McCann and Travis, blending in real good, like a couple of buffalo in a herd of deer. I didn't know why they were there; I thought maybe you had sent them."

"Your problems with your ex-wife had nothing to do with me at that point, Michael. And I wouldn't use those two incompetents, anyway. It was probably another case of them imagining they had something besides fluff between their ears."

Minghella nodded seriously. "I've told them before – just do what you're told to do. Don't think. Anyway, I wasn't sure whether to go ahead or not. I was watching Shirley when she came into the restaurant with Romano, and they sat down at a table. I supposed she was using him as cover. I was all set to make like it was a chance meeting of old friends, but then Shirley says something to Romano, and he takes off. What the hell was I supposed to think?"

"You're not supposed to think, either," Innes said. "That's my department."

Minghella took that on the chin, which impressed Zukie. She wondered if the two men even remembered she was there.

"Then I saw McCann take off after Romano, so I figured that side of things was covered. I closed in on Shirley and told her to give me the replica and she said she didn't have it. She'd changed her mind."

Zukie could guess out what had happened after that. McCann – who was either Len or the driver – had sideswiped Lou in the parking garage, but hadn't been able to search him and retrieve the fake *netsuke* because he hadn't been badly injured and there were too many people watching. And of course, Lou hadn't known Shirley had planted it on him.

"I figured she'd given it to Romano for safe-keeping and was planning to get it back later and go to the cops," Minghella said. "I told her she had twenty-four hours to get it back to me."

"And we know how well that worked out," Innes said. "She went straight to the cops and then one or both of those two jerks broke into her condo, dragged her out and shot her. Not content with that, they had to trash Romano's car and try to break into his house. Did it never occur to either them or you that Romano didn't have the damn replica? God knows where it is now, but I'm betting the cops have it, and that will bring them straight back to you. And then to me. Michael, you are a good artist and a reasonably competent thief, but as a judge of human nature, you're a total idiot. And tell me, why are those two still loose on the street?"

193

Minghella didn't have an answer. Zukie could understand that.

"Then as if they hadn't screwed up enough, they go and snatch her." Innes gestured at Zukie.

"Yeah. You want me to get rid of her?"

They both contemplated Zukie, who tried hard not to look as though her fate was being decided.

"It's too late for that," Innes said.

NOT FAR from the edge of Innes's property, several vehicles had pulled into place, blocking exits from the estate and waiting for a signal. On the lake, hovering just beyond the sightline from his dock, a police boat was idling. Had she known this, Zukie would have been flattered that she merited so much attention.

If she had, Vance, in the lead car, would have informed her tersely that she was just a cog in the machinery and that the main goal of the operation was to solve a homicide case and crack a major art theft ring. Rescuing a nosy civilian who had shoved her way into the investigation and been kidnapped as a result was only a minor side issue.

Minghella's car had gone past them just after Vance arrived, and Holt had immediately checked the plate and relayed the owner's name.

"Two for the price of one," Vance said approvingly. "Innes is the brains behind the racket but Minghella is the guy on the ground. This could work out well, assuming Innes isn't planning to use her as collateral."

"And assuming Innes isn't planning to dispose of Minghella, who after all, has become a major liability. Have they got McCann and Travis yet?"

Lanigan kept scanning the woods as he spoke, half expecting Zukie to come running through the trees, possibly pursued by someone with a gun.

Vance listened to what Holt was telling them and repeated it to Lanigan.

"Yes. Picked them up on East Marginal at the plastics factory. Along with a black Ford sedan which may be the one that hit Romano."

Lanigan heaved a silent sigh of relief. He knew Zukie wasn't yet out of the woods – quite literally – but he felt a little better knowing Minghella's two henchmen weren't holding her.

"OK," Vance said into his mouthpiece. "Everybody set? Let's get this show on the road."

ZUKIE wasn't sure whether to be relieved or alarmed at Innes's comment. She almost wished she'd been sent out of the room while the two men talked, even though their conversation hadn't revealed much that she didn't already know or had guessed. And if they were telling the truth, neither of them was directly responsible for Shirley's death.

They were both now looking at her, as if deciding whether to dump her in the lake or possibly bury her in the woods somewhere. She looked straight back at them, hoping Minghella might have retained some sort of ethnic reluctance to murder a fellow Italian, especially a woman. He frowned at her.

"I know you," he said. "You used to work at the Plane View, didn't you?"

"That's right." Zukie happily seized the chance to find some common ground. "I quit a couple of years ago when my husband died. You know, I thought you looked kind of familiar. Did you used to eat there?"

"Yeah, once in a while."

"Can we skip the reunion?" Innes said irritably. "We've got a problem here. As I said, Michael, the time has come for us to part ways."

Zukie wasn't sure what that implied, but it didn't sound good. Minghella must have agreed, because he half rose from his chair.

"Sit down," Innes ordered him.

"I know I made some mistakes, but I'm not that stupid," Minghella said. "You'll never find anyone who can make replicas like me."

"I appreciate your skills, Michael. But you do realize the cops will finger you for ordering your ex-wife's murder. That's unacceptable."

"But I didn't." Minghella was still sitting, but on the very edge of the chair. Innes stood up. Zukie sucked in her breath, and as she did, the intercom buzzed insistently.

Innes cursed under his breath and strode over to it. "Yes?"

"A car just went through. We couldn't stop them."

"What do you mean, you couldn't stop them? You've got a gun."

"They had a search warrant."

Innes slammed the intercom off and glared at Minghella.

"You double-crossed me, Michael."

Minghella glared back. "I did not. I don't know who's there, but I had nothing to do with it."

"Then it was probably your two idiots, leaving a trail a deaf, dumb and blind man could follow."

Zukie certainly hoped that was the case. Someone with a search warrant sounded like someone she could look forward to seeing. Innes and Minghella were still scowling at one another, and Minghella acted first, probably on the theory that Innes would have a firearm not too far away.

He swung a fist that knocked Innes onto one of the sofas, but Innes leaped back up and head-butted him. Minghella shook his head as if dislodging something from his ears and Innes dropped into a crouch. They circled each other warily, while Zukie wondered if they would notice if she slipped out the door.

The sound of a vehicle approaching came from outside. Innes flicked a glance at the window, then at Minghella and finally at Zukie, who was edging toward the door.

"It must be her they're after," he said through gritted teeth. "Your two goons had to bring her here, didn't they? So let's use her as a shield and we'll both get out. They won't risk shooting her. I'll deal with you later."

Zukie didn't like the sound of that. She doubted she could

evade or outrun both of them, and she had no desire to get caught in the crossfire if shooting was on the agenda. She froze for a nanosecond and then darted back between the two men and across the room.

Before either man could react, she had grabbed the little ivory fish from the shelf and leaped for the door, Innes a couple of yards behind her. He was shouting something, but she wasn't about to stop and listen. She knew he would catch her before any law enforcement officers could get to her, and she didn't want to think about what would happen then.

There was only one thing to do.

She streaked across the terrace, drew back her arm and threw the *netsuke* into the koi pond.

Chapter 20

Vance had been planning to create a distraction, but when he saw Zukie run out of the house, he rapidly realized he didn't need to. She raced past the fish pond, dodged around the police car and hurled herself under the low-hanging Japanese maple, while Innes gave a howl of anguish and skidded to a halt by the koi.

"Come on," Vance said, as two more cars pulled up behind his and the island officers piled out. "Find Minghella. He'll be in the house somewhere. Lanigan, get Mrs Merlino out from under that tree. I'll deal with Innes."

From her vantage point under the maple's feathery leaves, Zukie watched as Vance approached Innes. He was frantically peering into the pond, and she couldn't tell whether he was trying to locate the *netsuke* or check whether any of his fish had been knocked out when she threw it into the water.

She dimly heard Vance say, "Clement Innes? Detective Lee Vance, Seattle Police Department ..."

"My fish," Innes said plaintively. "If any of my fish have been injured ..."

"... suspicion of possession of stolen goods. You have the right to remain silent ..."

Zukie curled up and hoped no one would notice her,

especially not Minghella, if he had left the house before the police found him. A face appeared at the edge of the leaves and she cringed, but it was a friendly one.

Lanigan said, "You can come out now, Zukie."

She uncurled herself and crawled out, brushing leaves off her hair and clothes and straightening her wig. She stood up and was glad to note her legs weren't trembling.

"Jeez, I'm glad to see you, Jim."

"Likewise. I'll call Lou and tell him you're all right. He was absolutely frantic."

"Lou doesn't do frantic."

"You could have fooled me. Very concerned, then."

Lanigan took out his phone and called. Zukie could hear Lou on the other end demanding, "Are you sure she's OK?"

She snatched the phone from Lanigan and said, "Yes, Lou, I'm fine. Jim's got work to do now. Bye." She turned back to Lanigan. "Where is this place, anyway?"

"Mercer Island. Those guys are MI cops. It's really their show, although since most of the criminal activity took place in Seattle, we're sharing information."

"And the credit for taking those two down."

She stood by the maple and watched as officers escorted a handcuffed Minghella to one of the cars. Innes, still complaining about his fish being mistreated, was placed in another one. They drove off and Vance came over to Zukie.

"Are you all right, Mrs Merlino?"

"Yeah, I think so. He kind of twisted my wrist at one point, 'cause I fibbed to him about Lou, but otherwise he didn't do anything to me. And he gave me a sandwich and a couple cups of real good coffee."

Lanigan fought to keep his face straight. He could just imagine Zukie recounting her experience in a courtroom and declaring that Innes should be cut some slack because he had fed her.

"What did you throw into the fish pond?" Vance asked.

"Oh, that. An antique ivory *netsuke*. The fish one. It's

probably worth a lot of money. I wouldn't have done it, but I figured it was the one thing he would stop and look for. I hope you can find it without draining the pond, 'cause he's real attached to his fish."

"We noticed," Lanigan said.

"And I sure hope none of the fish swallowed it."

"We'll find it somehow," Vance said. "And then we'll return it to its rightful owner."

"Yeah, he as much as said it wasn't his. Or rather, Minghella did. He stole things to order for him and then put real good copies in their place. Did you know that?"

"Yes, or at least we had surmised that's what was happening. Innes is a genuine collector all right, but he comes unhinged when there's something he wants and can't buy legitimately."

Zukie nodded. "He's got a lot of stuff in there," she said, indicating the house. "Some of it's real nice, but I wonder how much of it is really his."

"That's something for the art theft detail to work out. They'll check his collection against a database of reported stolen items. Meanwhile, let's get you back to the precinct and you can tell us what happened here."

IT WAS several hours later when Zukie finally finished telling Vance the complete story of her abduction, lightly skipping over the fact that if she had been minding her own business, she would never have been a target in the first place.

"Guess it was just bad luck I happened to be where McCann and Travis spotted me, wasn't it?" she asked.

"McCann and Travis are what's euphemistically called security officers for Minghella Plastics," Vance said. "As such, they're usually somewhere on the premises, and also run little errands for Michael Minghella when he needs some extra muscle and doesn't want to get his own hands dirty."

"So it wasn't just bad luck. Did one of them shoot Shirley?"

Vance exchanged glances with Lanigan.

"We have a strong suspicion ..."

"That means they did," Zukie said, nodding. "They're not very bright, you know, and from what Clem said, they sometimes decide to do things on their own. When we were driving over the bridge, I heard them say something about snatching someone because she was nothing but trouble. Well, of course, I thought they meant me."

"As you would," Vance couldn't help saying.

"Yeah, but I don't think they were. I think the same thing happened before – that they grabbed Shirley 'cause it seemed like a good idea at the time, and then they didn't know what to do once they had her. Clem wouldn't have wanted her brought over there any more than he wanted me there, and Michael didn't want to anyone connecting him with her. If they'd just turned her loose, she'd have gone straight to you guys. They were stuck. Couldn't go forward, couldn't go back. So they killed her, which was the worst possible thing they could have done."

"Yes."

"Sort of like Henry and Thomas Becket."

"Pardon?" Vance wondered briefly if there were two other people involved in the case that he hadn't heard about. "Who are they?"

Zukie shook her head at the ignorance of the police force.

"King Henry, back in the twelfth century, I think it was, saying something about wanting to be rid of this troublesome priest. He didn't really mean he wanted Becket dead, but some helpful knights took things into their own hands and killed him.

"Henry wasn't very happy about that and I don't think Michael Minghella was very happy about Shirley being killed, either. He'd probably said she was causing trouble for him and so Len and his friend thought they'd be real helpful. Becket was murdered in a cathedral. Where was Shirley found?"

Vance looked a little dazed. It was hard enough to follow Zukie's thought process in the current century, let alone through a 900-year detour.

"In the parking lot by the Plane View restaurant."

"Oh, jeez. Does Lou know that?"

"No."

"I won't tell him, 'cause he goes there a lot and he wouldn't want to if he knew that. They must have brought her there from wherever she was living."

"Yes," Vance said.

"It appears," Lanigan said, "as if they broke into her condo, maybe trying to find anything that might incriminate Minghella. But as you noted, they're not very good at burglary, either. She managed to set off her security alarm before they hustled her out of there, and because she fought back, either she or they managed to break a window."

"Why didn't you tell me and Lou that? You made it sound like she was killed in her house or condo or whatever. Shot through a window, you said. Sheesh."

"Because," Vance said bluntly, "at that point, we weren't completely sure Mr Romano wasn't involved. Men have been known to act totally out of character when a woman's in the picture. And she had his name and cell phone number on a scrap of paper in her pocket."

"Oh. I wondered how you connected him to her."

"For what it's worth, Zukie," Lanigan said, "I think Shirley genuinely liked Lou."

"Well, he's not a bad guy," Zukie said judiciously. "And from what Minghella said, she didn't set him up to get run over at the mall, either. That was the two brainboxes thinking they could get the fake *netsuke* off him in the parking garage. That was about the only thing they got right, figuring out that Shirley had planted it on him. But some Good Samaritan got there first and called 911, so they didn't have a chance to roll him. Are you going to get them for attempted murder on top of everything else?"

"The charge of first-degree homicide will take precedence," Vance said. "Then there's kidnapping, assault, vandalism, burglary ... the list goes on."

"How about Minghella?"

"The art theft people are working on it. I'm sure they will come up with something."

"Good. And Innes?"

"That's going to be a little harder, since he has always managed to stay one step removed. But it's safe to say his art collection will be scrutinized to see how much of it actually belongs to him and what doesn't. He could be an accessory to the thefts, or in possession of stolen goods, if nothing else."

Zukie nodded. "He did apologize to me."

"Oh, well," Lanigan said. "That makes it all right, then."

A FEW days later, Zukie was playing on her living room floor with Joe. She had a plastic ball, which she was rolling to him, and he was trying to grab it when it came within reach. Lou was on the sofa, watching them with amusement.

"Here you go, Joe," she said, rolling the ball. Joe made a dive for it, landing on his chin. He struggled back up, his eyes never leaving the ball.

"Good boy," Lou said. "Keep trying, and one of these times you'll get it right. Jesus, Mary and Joseph."

"Hush," Zukie said sharply. "What's the matter with you, Lou? It's only a ball."

"Shirley. That's what she told me to remember."

"Huh?"

Joe had managed to work his way over to the ball. He gave it a push and it rolled past Zukie, who absently put a hand out to stop it.

"On the postcard."

"She told you to keep trying and you'd get it right? Doesn't sound very complimentary to me."

"She meant," Lou said patiently, "that someday I might meet someone special. She knew it wasn't her."

"Why not? You're a nice guy."

"Thanks, Zuke, but that's not the point. Shirley was out of my league. I liked her real well, but it was never going to work long term and we both knew it. That's why I didn't bother saying anything to you about her."

"Oh. So that message wasn't anything about Japanese antiques?"

"Of course not. When we went to the museum, that was a good example. She loved it and I was bored stiff."

"So what you want is to meet someone who likes baseball, Italian food and bowling."

Whatever Lou might have replied was lost as the doorbell rang. Zukie made a gesture indicating he should answer it, as she scrambled to her feet and picked Joe up.

"Thanks," she heard Lou say.

"What's that?"

"Damned if I know." Lou was holding up a carton about a foot on each side. "It's marked 'fragile' and ... 'live'?"

"Better open it up, Lou. Carefully."

Lou obeyed and looked inside. He stared, and then chortled. "You won't believe this, Zuke."

"What is it?"

He pulled the carton loose and dropped it, revealing a clear glass globe. It was two-thirds filled with water and swimming in the water were two small orange and white fish.

"Good grief," Zukie said. "Who sends goldfish through the mail?" Even as she said it, she knew the answer. "Oh, my God. I bet they're from Clem."

Lou set the bowl down on the coffee table and removed a card from the wrapping paper.

"Good guess."

He read it out: *"With apologies for my lack of hospitality. Don't worry – these two won't get much bigger. C.I."*

Zukie stared at the fish.

"I never had a pet before. Oh, aren't they cute? Look, Joe. Pretty orange fishies. I think I'll call one Clem and the other .... Clementine."

"How do you know one's a male and one's a female?"

"I don't. Would you rather I called them Lou and Shirley?"
Lou sighed and looked at the fish bowl.
"Hi, Clem. Hi, Clementine."

Thank you for reading *Zukie's Thief*. If you enjoyed it, please tell your friends and leave a review! You can also join Zukie and Lou on their other adventures:

Zukie's Burglar (Zukie Merlino Mysteries 1)

Having lost both her husband and her job, Zukie Merlino has time on her hands and a mystery to solve. Night after night, someone is searching the empty house next door, whose elderly owner died following an unusually explosive Fourth of July. A second death in the house brings out all Zukie's detective instincts, and with the help of her reluctant accomplice Lou, she launches her own investigation, using her wits, her wigs and a coffee cake or two.

Zukie's Witness (Zukie Merlino Mysteries 2)

Teenager Austin Barrett made a big mistake when he tried to mug Zukie Merlino, but now he's on the run after witnessing a murder and he needs her help. And why not? Whether it's helping her friends at the delicatessen to corner an olive oil shoplifter or tracking down a killer who seems to have vanished into thin air, Zukie is always willing to put her *pasta e fagioli* on the back burner and apply her detective skills to solving a mystery.

Zukie's Suspect (Zukie Merlino Mysteries 3)

Everybody liked good-natured Jimmy Battista, so when he died of a heart attack, no one suspected foul play. No one, that is, except his elderly sister-in-law, who confided her suspicions to her niece Zukie. Being seriously snoopy and a magnet for trouble, Zukie is soon up to her multi-colored wigs in a mystery involving Italian relatives, a German shepherd and a Canadian corpse.

Zukie's Detective (Zukie Merlino Mysteries 4)

A chance to win $10,000 by writing a fast food slogan seems like a no-brainer to Zukie Merlino, but things go disastrously wrong when one of her co-competitors is murdered at the hotel where they're all staying for the final round. Confined to quarters but still able to cause chaos, Zukie discovers something nasty in the fish pond, shares her bedroom with a strange man and worst of all, is forced to eat someone else's cooking.

Zukie's Alibi (Zukie Merlino Mysteries 5)

Back from the vacation of a lifetime, Zukie Merlino finds it hard to readjust to her daily routine, so she's pleased to receive an invitation to her high school reunion. Not only will it break the boredom but give her the chance to confront Sylvia, a woman she's hated for years. Away from her cousin Lou's disapproving eyes for once, Zukie is enjoying herself greatly at the reunion, at least until Sylvia's body is discovered in the parking lot. Zukie knows she's not guilty, but the only way of proving her innocence is by providing an alibi she doesn't want to give.

Zukie's Evidence (Zukie Merlino Mysteries 6)

A young woman falls to her death in a crowded shopping mall during the Black Friday sales frenzy. Her family think it must have been a tragic accident. The police suspect it was suicide. But Zukie Merlino thinks Mimi Carr was murdered, and she sets out to prove it, with the reluctant assistance of her cousin Lou. Will some leftover turkey, a parking ticket and a pair of high-heeled boots be convincing enough evidence?

Zukie's Promise (Zukie Merlino Mysteries 7)

Zukie Merlino's daughter Carol is (finally) getting married, and Zukie has been told in no uncertain terms that her role at the wedding is to show up, shut up and keep smiling. That's hard enough, but when a body turns up at the rehearsal, she faces an even tougher challenge. The wedding's in two days; the bride and groom are suspected of murder and everyone involved seems to be hiding a secret. But Zukie has promised herself nothing will ruin Carol's wedding, and Zukie always keeps her promises, no matter whose toes she has to step on along the way.

Zukie's Trail (Zukie Merlino Mysteries 8)

Most people would jump at the chance of a free, relaxing vacation on a picturesque island, but not Zukie Merlino, to whom 'rest' is a four-letter word. Her outlook improves, however, when there's a death at the rustic inn where she's a reluctant guest. Despite the best efforts of her cousin Lou and the local law enforcement officers, Zukie is soon hot on the trail of a murderer, a task that sees her commandeering the inn's kitchen, stealing a boat and getting a lot closer to the great outdoors than she ever anticipated.

Zukie's Ghost (Zukie Merlino Mysteries 9)

Twenty years ago, Gus Novak committed a crime and fled the country, only to die in the Mexican desert. But Zukie Merlino thinks she's just seen him on a downtown Seattle street, and being perpetually curious, she wants to know what he – or his ghost – is doing there. With her cousin Lou temporarily sidelined she's on her own, but whether it's tracking down Novak's ghost or dealing with a more personal emergency, Zukie can be counted on to deliver the goods.

Also by Cynthia E. Hurst:

In 1860s Oxfordshire, two outsiders -- a Jewish clock repairer and a thief turned housemaid -- team up to solve mysteries in the **Silver and Simm Victorian Mysteries** series.

Tools of the Trade (Silver and Simm Victorian Mysteries 1)
Forged in the Fire (Silver and Simm Victorian Mysteries 2)
Writing on the Wall (Silver and Simm Victorian Mysteries 3)
Stitched up in Style (Silver and Simm Victorian Mysteries 4)
Ghost on the Green (Silver and Simm Victorian Mysteries 5)

Set in Seattle, the **R&P Labs Mysteries** feature a quintet of scientists with a knack for solving mysteries, matched only by their ability to stumble over them in the first place.

Mossfire (R&P Labs Mysteries 1)
Sweetwater (R&P Labs Mysteries 2)
Shellshock (R&P Labs Mysteries 3)
Angelwood   (R&P Labs Mysteries 4)
Boneflower (R&P Labs Mysteries 5)
Childproof   (R&P Labs Mysteries 6)
Dreamwheel (R&P Labs Mysteries 7)
Icefox (R&P Labs Mysteries 8)
Shotglass (R&P Labs Mysteries 9)
Pushover (R&P Labs Mysteries 10)
Bedrock (R&P Labs Mysteries 11)
Uprooted (R&P Labs Mysteries 12)
Four by Five (R&P Labs Mysteries short stories)

Printed in Great Britain
by Amazon